FEAR ON THE LEVELS

A gripping crime thriller full of suspense

DAVID HODGES

(Detective Kate Hamblin mystery book 3)

JOFFE BOOKS

Revised edition 2019
Joffe Books, London
www.joffebooks.com

First published in Great Britain 2015 as "Strawfoot"

We hate typos too but sometimes they slip through.
Please send any errors you find to
corrections@joffebooks.com
We'll get them fixed ASAP. We're very grateful to eagle-eyed readers who take the time to contact us.

Please join our mailing list for free Kindle crime thriller, detective, mystery books and new releases.
http://www.joffebooks.com/contact/
ISBN: 978-1-78931-121-1

DEDICATION

This book is dedicated to my wife, Elizabeth, for all her love, patience and support over so many wonderful years and to my late mother and father, whose faith in me to one day achieve my ambition as a writer remained steadfast throughout their lifetime and whose tragic passing has left a hole in my life that will never be filled.

AUTHOR'S NOTE

ALTHOUGH THE ACTION of this novel takes place in the Avon & Somerset police area, the story itself and all the characters in it are entirely fictitious. Similarly, at the time of writing, there is *no* police station in Highbridge. This has been drawn entirely from the author's imagination to ensure no connection is made between any existing police station or personnel in the force and the content of the novel. I would also point out that I have used some poetic licence in relation to the local police structure and some of the specific procedures followed by Avon & Somerset Police in order to meet the requirements of the plot. Nevertheless, the policing background depicted in the novel is broadly in accord with the national picture and these little departures from fact will, hopefully, not spoil the reading enjoyment of serving or retired police officers for whom I have the utmost respect. Finally, I would add that scarecrow festivals actually do take place in various villages throughout Somerset during the course of each year and it may be of interest to my readers to know that it was the imaginative display of these sinister figures in a line of driveways and gardens as I was driving home one gloomy evening that provided me with the inspiration for this novel and raised the question that is forever in the mind of every fiction writer: 'What if. . . ?'

David Hodges

BEFORE THE FACT

Somerset Levels, 1863

GHOST LIGHTS. BOBBING eerily in the dank mist that choked the Somerset Levels like balls of iridescent bog cotton. Blurred figures moving wraith-like along the drove. Voices calling hoarsely to each other, fear lacing their tone, as if each took comfort from the presence of the other.

'Jeremiah, d'ye see anything, man?'

A marsh bird rose from among the reeds to Tom Draycott's right with a startled cry but there was no response from his friend and neighbour. Fearing the 60-year-old withy worker might have missed his footing and fallen into the rhyne bordering the track, Tom was about to shout again when the faint disembodied reply drifted back to him on the clouds of mist. 'Nay, Tom but keep looking. The wench must be near.'

On the other side of the rhyne, Jeremiah Tinney licked his lips nervously, wiping away the fine drizzle streaming down his thin weather-beaten face with one arthritic hand. Martha – his only daughter – was always home before this. It was but a short walk to their isolated cottage along the drove from the inn on the outskirts of Westhay where she worked in the evenings and she was never this late. Would that Martha's mother had still been alive, then maybe the girl's wayward nature might have been curtailed. Jeremiah was tired of trying to tame her himself. The belt had achieved nothing – it had only made her more stubborn – and, from what he'd heard, she seemed to take a delight in flaunting herself in front of the inn's rough customers as she replenished their pint pots with local cider, shaming not only herself but her own father as well. And now she had gone missing and was heaven alone knew where.

Jeremiah stopped a few seconds to relight his pipe, which had succumbed to the damp, sucking on the badly chewed stem until the tobacco reluctantly fizzed into life and the heady smoke filled his nostrils. 'Where you be, girl?' he muttered, squinting into the mist. ''Taint a night to be out on the marsh.'

A gnarled shape loomed suddenly in the gloom and he caught his breath, choking on the smoke from the pipe. It was only a stunted alder tree but it had given him quite a start, thoughts of demons and other unmentionables crowding his weary brain.

The Levels abounded with legends of witches, goblins and marsh sprites and, even though the old man counted himself a level-headed practical soul – a pillar of his local church – on a night like this, it was easy to be seduced into believing anything.

He remembered the gypsy crone who had called at his cottage only that afternoon, her eyes like gimlets and her lip curling with venom when he had refused to buy her clothes pegs. 'A curse on ye,' she'd snarled. 'Bad luck will be yours for this.' Peeping down at her from her bedroom window, Martha had mocked the old woman cruelly, calling her a withered old derelict, and she had responded with a stab of one claw-like finger. 'Ol' Strawfoot will come for ye, my beauty, that I promise. And then ye'll be sorry.'

Jeremiah shivered and gripped his pipe more tightly between his clenched teeth. Nonsense, he mused. Strawfoot was just a stupid story with which the old maids frightened errant children. 'Be good, or Strawfoot will take you away,' they warned gleefully, eliciting instant obedience. Well, Jeremiah Tinney was not a child. He was an honest God-fearing man and no foolish superstition about spectral scarecrows was going to get to *him*.

He saw the derelict barn a few moments later and crossed the ploughed field towards it, his boots squelching in the furrows. Tom was already there and together they hauled the pair of heavy doors open and cast their lanterns around the interior.

They saw her immediately. She was lying on her back in a corner, naked from the waist down, her body inert and strangely contorted, and the bulging sightless eyes and distorted lips, peeled back in a silent choking scream, testifying to the horrific ordeal she had been subjected to. And, as if this wasn't enough, as a final cruel ignominy, a small straw doll had been forced into her mouth over her protruding tongue, like a grotesque infant pacifier.

For a moment Jeremiah simply stood there, frozen to the spot by the horrific discovery, his pipe dropping from his mouth to the floor, the tobacco cascading from the bowl as the burning embers hissed to extinction in the damp mud. Then, very slowly, barely aware of Tom's muttered prayer as he crossed himself or the tramp of feet as the rest of the small search party entered the barn behind them, he bent down beside the twisted corpse of his beloved daughter to take one limp hand in his own. 'What in God's name—' he blurted with a choking cry.

'God?' another rough voice cut in harshly. 'God had nothing to do with this, Jeremiah. It be the devil's work.' And as the light of the speaker's lantern fell on the bare floor in front of the dead girl's feet, the old man noticed for the first time the trail of straw leading across the barn to disappear into the mist billowing in through the open door. ''Tis the work of ol' Strawfoot hisself.'

And as he spoke, the heavy doors behind them stirred uneasily under a sudden inexplicable blast of cold air and something scrabbled along the outside of the barn with talon-like fingers.

CHAPTER 1

EXACTLY 150 YEARS after the murder of Martha Tinney, the mist once again billowed across the Somerset Levels, quickly devouring the sodden marshland and the lattice-work of rivers and rhynes that fed this vast wetland habitat and extinguishing the winking lights of the cottages and wayside hostelries as effectively as a massive power cut. The white clouds rolled all the way out to the M5 motorway to the magical hump of Brent Knoll, completely blotting out the villages that crouched in its path. It imposed a sepulchral stillness over everything, a stillness that was broken only by the plaintive bleating of sheep and the sound of the cows in the waterlogged fields tugging at the long grass – and, very occasionally, as fuzzy headlights emerged from the gloom, the rumble of a slow-running engine when a car or lorry nosed onwards.

Melanie Schofield's high-heeled boots tapping out their steady rhythm on the patched tarmac sounded strangely loud and intrusive as she headed home but the quick sharp steps also communicated the fury that continued to grip the young brunette even after half an hour of rapid walking.

The left side of her face was still sore from the slap her boyfriend, Ed Shearing, had given her – in response to the one she had dealt him – and, despite her anger at the way he had treated her, she had difficulty holding back the tears. To find him upstairs in bed with that blonde tart was bad enough but then to be thrown out of his friend's house with the party still in full swing and left to face the long solitary walk home at past eleven at night was just unbelievable.

It was creepy on the lonely road too. The annual scarecrow festival was underway in the village and the grotesque straw figures, dressed by the locals in their outlandish costumes, had given her quite a start when they'd first loomed up in the mist – some sitting astride garden walls, others standing like grim sentinels from another world on verges and in driveway entrances. More than once she'd thought she had seen one move, maybe wave a tattered arm or nod a turnip head in sombre greeting – half expecting to see the thing ease itself off its perch or tug its supporting pole out of the grass to stumble after her with jerky robot-like steps.

She shivered, pausing a moment to wipe away her tears on the sleeve of her coat and cursing Ed through gritted teeth for abandoning her in such a scary place. She promised herself that she would tell her big brother, Dan, what the arsehole had done to her the first chance she got and her mouth twisted into a vindictive sneer as she savoured the anticipated outcome. Shearing would not be so full of himself after Dan had paid him a visit, that was for sure, and his new bimbo girlfriend would soon lose her hots for 'lover-boy' once she had seen the extent to which his face had been rearranged.

Then abruptly Melanie's sneer froze on her smudged lipstick and she jerked around to peer back into the mist, shaken out of her reverie by what she thought was the sound of footsteps a short distance behind her. But she saw nothing save swirling white vapour, forming, parting, then re-forming in serpentine twists and twirls, like a multitude of smoky questing tongues.

Frowning, she moved on, her shivering becoming more acute as the damp crept up her thighs from the road surface through her tight jeans and her throat started to burn in the raw stagnant air drifting in off the marsh.

The old stone houses watched her from behind their gates, silent and brooding, as she passed by – a couple still leaching ghostly light through gaps in the curtains drawn across the windows of their upstairs bedrooms – and the tap of her heels was thrown backwards and forwards between their high walls in dull flat echoes.

But then she had turned off the main drag into a narrow lane and the vague outline of the marsh was opening up ahead of her. Shortly afterwards, there was nothing but fences and skeletal hedgerows, with the branches of stunted trees reaching over them towards her like curled fingers. A car passed her, heading out of the village, slowing briefly at the last minute as it caught her shadow in its headlights before it was gone and she was alone again.

Moisture dripped on to her face from an overhanging branch and it was only when she stopped a second to wipe one eye clear that she heard the footfalls again and this time, when she turned a little more quickly, she thought she caught a glimpse of something among the swirling clouds of vapour – a dark shape, tall and thin but appearing disembodied, like a phantom, in the gloom. Then it was gone as abruptly as it had appeared, swallowed up by the mist as if it had never existed in the first place. Probably hadn't either, she thought ruefully; just the Levels playing tricks on her.

She heard nothing else after that save the tap of her high heels, but finally turning into the long driveway leading up to the old farmhouse she had called home for the past eighteen years, she imagined something flitted across the driveway in front of her – again indistinct and disembodied but resembling an upright male figure, dressed in a long tattered-looking coat and floppy hat – like one of the scarecrows she had passed on the main drag. Bloody hell, girl, she mused, what *is* the matter with you? Seeing straw men following you? Too much red wine at the party tonight, that's for sure. You're home now, so get a grip.

Her house keys were in her hand before she reached the front door and she grimaced when she saw that there were no cars in the gravel parking area. Damn, her parents were obviously still out and her brother had told her he wasn't likely to be back from his gig in Taunton until after midnight anyway. Just her luck.

Then she saw the glow in the murk to her right and frowned. The barn: someone had left the lights on in the barn. Her mood brightened. The motorbike – Dan was obviously back earlier than he had expected and was working on the thing again, as he often did until the early hours, bloody idiot!

Turning on her heel, she headed towards the light, relieved that big brother was on hand and keen to unload her night of misery on him at the earliest opportunity. Yeah, Dan would sort Ed out after what he had done, no question; Dan would give him a right hiding.

The barn doors stood wide open and the distinctive workshop smell of the place hit her even before she stepped inside – a combination of oil, petrol and paint-spray that always made her wrinkle her nose in disgust when it greeted her. 'Dan?' she called. 'You'll never guess—'

But she never finished the sentence. Dan's old Triumph Bonneville motorcycle was there all right, partially stripped and standing in a pool of oil a few yards from her father's Massey Ferguson tractor and rusted baler but there was no sign of Dan.

Feeling more than a little apprehensive but suspecting that her brother had heard her coming and was hiding behind the farm machinery, preparing to jump out on her when she got closer – as he had on numerous occasions before – she stopped short beside the motorcycle and stared around the barn.

'Dan!' she called again, now more than a little frightened. 'This isn't funny. Where are you?'

Something – possibly a rat – scampered away among the bales of straw stacked on the other side of the barn and she heard the soft whinnying of the two horses in the stable next door, followed by the nervous stamping of hoofs.

'Dan!' she snapped, suddenly angry again. 'You're pissing me off. I'm going indoors.'

She heard the rustling sound almost at the same moment and, turning quickly, was startled to see a tall dark figure framed in the open doorway behind her – a figure that stood there as motionless as a statue, studying her with a silent unwavering intensity. In the long ragged coat and floppy hat, from under which stalks of straw protruded, it looked a lot like Worzel Gummidge but this wasn't Worzel Gummidge – and it wasn't her brother, Dan, either.

CHAPTER 2

DETECTIVE SERGEANT KATE Lewis stomped into the CID office at Highbridge police station at nine in the morning, her freckled face pale and drawn through lack of sleep, ageing her beyond her thirty years, and her shoulder-length auburn hair needing an energetic brushing.

'Kate?' the office manager acknowledged from his desk in the corner, his gaze flicking briefly towards her, then back to the bar chart on his computer screen. 'Good honeymoon, was it?'

She threw him a hard glance and made straight for the coffee machine, thinking sourly of her wedding just two weeks before and the catastrophe that had wrecked her Seychelles honeymoon, resulting in the repatriation of new hubby, Hayden, straight to Taunton hospital with a back injury.

'Don't start, Dick,' she snapped. 'I'm not in the mood!'

A former detective sergeant like Kate before his retirement five years before, Dick Stacey was not so easily put off. 'So how's the casualty then?' he persisted, still studying his computer screen but now wearing a broad grin. 'Damage any important muscles, did he?'

Kate turned to face him, sipping her coffee, her blue eyes narrowed and wary. 'Hayden hurt his back, that's all,' she said coldly. 'Fell down some steps at the hotel, OK? They think he's cracked his pelvis and are keeping him in for a day or so to run some tests.'

Stacey chuckled. 'As long as he hasn't cracked anything else. Jumping off those foreign wardrobes can be pretty lethal.'

Kate grimaced but ignored the remark. 'Where is everybody?' she queried instead.

Stacey pushed himself away from the desk and swung round in his swivel chair to face her. His smile had gone now and his expression was serious. 'Missing eighteen-year-old,' he said. 'Didn't return home after a night out with her boyfriend.'

Kate frowned. 'Old enough at eighteen, isn't she? We don't usually get involved with adult mispers so early. She's probably over the side with someone.'

He nodded. 'You're all heart, Kate,' he said. 'Uniform aren't happy, though. Local community support officer knows the family well and says it's completely out of character.' He hesitated. 'Also, her dad used to be on the local Bench.'

Kate treated him to a cynical smile. 'Ah, now that explains it all. Nepotism still rules OK, does it?'

He shrugged and turned back to his screen. 'Maybe but DC Ashton has gone over there to take a look – DI Roscoe's orders.'

'And where *is* Mr Roscoe?' she queried. 'I thought he'd still be in bed.'

'No, he's not, Sergeant,' a deep voice growled almost at her elbow. 'He's right behind you.'

Kate winced and turned slowly to face the speaker, leaving Stacey to choke into the mug of coffee on his desk.

The stocky balding man in the dark grey overcoat and pork-pie hat who stood there looked a bit like the soldier depicted on the First World War 'Join Your Country's Army' posters than a police detective inspector. His greying Stalin moustache and heavy jowls quivered in time to a rapid gum-chewing motion and his dark, boot-button eyes studied her almost balefully from under bushy brows that looked as though they had never been trimmed. Detective Inspector Ted Roscoe was a formidable-looking individual and, approaching thirty years' police service, the former marine was certainly not someone to trifle with – especially as he had recently set himself the task of giving up his addiction to cigarettes, which had not helped his truculent mood one little bit.

'Morning, Guv,' Kate said in a peculiar strangled voice. 'Didn't see you.'

Roscoe nodded, shifting the gum in his mouth to the other cheek. 'Obviously,' he said. 'And for your information, I've just been told that the missing girl has been found.'

Kate nodded. 'That's good,' she said.

'No, it isn't,' he snapped back. 'They found her lying behind her dad's tractor in the barn. She's evidently been stiffed!'

'Oh shit!' Kate breathed.

'Exactly,' the DI agreed. 'So get your coat.'

A uniformed constable stood on guard in front of the single strand of blue and white 'Police' tape, which had been strung across the entrance to Lark Farm. Maybe they were on an economy drive, Kate mused cynically as she watched him unclip it from one of the gateposts to allow Roscoe's old Honda Civic car through. Moments later, the DI swung in between a marked police Transit van and one of the department's new CID cars parked at the front of the house and Kate climbed out with a sense of relief. Ted Roscoe was not the smoothest of drivers and, due to that and the state of some of the lumpy patched roads criss-crossing the Levels, it had been an uncomfortable near-white-knuckle ride. She was not looking forward to repeating the experience when they returned to the police station later.

Yellow police crime scene tapes were in evidence across the open doorway of a Dutch barn to the right of the house and two horses peered curiously over adjacent stable doors in the block next door, seemingly savouring the fragile autumn sunlight that had replaced the mist of the previous night. Kate waited respectfully for Roscoe to free himself from the car's twisted seatbelt before heading over there with him.

Detective Constable Jimmy Ashton, unsurprisingly known to his colleagues as Ash, cut around from the side of the barn to meet them. 'SOCO and pathologist on their way, Guv,' he announced. 'Best access to avoid fouling up the scene is down here.'

He grinned at Kate, in spite of the circumstances, as he brushed past her to lead the way down the side of the building. 'How's Hayden's poor little muscle, skipper?' he chortled close to her ear.

Kate treated him to a short hard stare. 'About as good as yours will be if you keep on, Ash,' she murmured with a tight smile, only too well aware that the news of her husband's accident would already have been widely broadcast over the grapevine and the mickey-taking was only just beginning.

Ash, unabashed and still smirking faintly, led them to a small door at the rear of the barn and, after first donning plastic overshoes, they stepped inside.

The interior of the windowless building was lit by a pair of strip-lights. Bales of straw were stacked floor to roof on either side of the door and battered farm machinery, including a tractor, baler and a couple of trailers, occupied the far side. There was an old partially constructed Triumph motorcycle on a stand in the centre of the barn, with an open toolbox and what looked like a recently sprayed petrol tank on an oily floor littered with an assortment of spanners, wrenches and screwdrivers in front of it.

Ash, no longer smirking, led the way across the barn to the far corner. Even before they got there, the humped shape was clearly visible in between the two trailers, and Kate's mouth tightened.

The body was that of a young girl, plainly a teenager, lying in a contorted position against the wheel of one of the trailers. She was naked from the waist down and wearing just a blue blouse, which seemed to have been deliberately pulled up over her breasts. Her head was bent back at an impossible angle, her feet crooked and the toes curled under them, digging into the bare earth in her final agonies. Closer examination revealed severe bruising to her throat and a film of blood obscuring the pupils of her distended eyeballs, suggesting she had been strangled. But her brutal killer had gone a stage further, displaying a macabre sense of humour by forcing what looked like a tiny straw figure into her mouth over her protruding tongue.

'Merciful heavens!' Kate breathed.

Roscoe grunted. 'Not much mercy shown here,' he observed grimly and, bending over the corpse, peered closely at the dead girl's face. 'What the hell is that thing sticking out of her mouth?'

'Corn dolly,' Ash responded promptly.

'A what?'

Ash grimaced. 'Corn dolly,' he said. 'Sort of folklore thing, I believe. You see them at craft fairs.'

'Doesn't look like a dolly to me.'

'No, Guv, it's called that but there are all sorts of types. I think they used to make them to promote the harvest – something like that.'

'So why would someone stick one in a girl's mouth?'

'Dunno, Guv. It's weird.'

Roscoe grunted. 'You can say that again. Who found her?'

'Local uniform guy,' Ash said. 'Duncan Jones.'

'When?'

'About forty minutes ago. Carried out the usual misper premises search and spotted her immediately.'

'Where are her clothes?'

Ash flicked his head towards the other side of the barn. 'Over there among those bales of straw – coat, jeans, pants and a pair of knee-length boots. Killer obviously dumped them there on his way out and there's a trail of straw, obviously from his boots or shoes, leading to the main doors.'

Roscoe glanced briefly in the direction he indicated. 'Who identified the body?'

'The brother, Guv – a Daniel Schofield.'

'Anyone else living here?'

'Just the mother and father apparently.'

'Where are they all?'

'In the house. In a hell of a state.'

'Hardly surprising under the circumstances,' Kate put in drily.

'Not fit for interview then?' Roscoe queried.

Ash hesitated. 'Parents, I would say no,' he replied, 'but the brother seems a bit more resilient from what I've seen of him.'

'Resilient or guilty?'

Ash looked shocked. 'Can't see him doing his own sister in, Guv.'

'Can't you?' Roscoe growled. 'Do this job long enough, Ash, and you'll believe anyone is capable of anything.'

He turned towards the side door of the barn through which they had entered. 'Stay here to meet the SOCO team and the pathologist,' he directed over his shoulder. 'I'll be back shortly.'

Ash nodded and watched them leave before settling himself on to a nearby straw bale and shaking a cigarette out of a crumpled packet. It was going to be a long day; he could feel it in his water.

The arrival of Roscoe and Lewis seemed to have passed unnoticed by the owners of the property but they were evidently spotted as they approached the front door. The tall muscular young man in the faded blue jeans and checked short-sleeve shirt opened up before they got to the step. His clean-shaven face was pale and his shoulder-length fair hair had obviously not yet seen a brush or comb that morning.

'Daniel Schofield?' Roscoe said quietly, and flashed his warrant card. 'DI Roscoe and DS Lewis.'

The young man nodded and stepped aside to allow them into the house. 'You'll have to speak to me,' he mumbled. 'Mum and Dad are—' He broke off with a helpless shrug.

Roscoe removed his pork-pie hat and held it against his chest as they both accepted the invitation and stepped through the doorway into a square hallway with internal doors opening off on three sides. Indicating a door on the left, Schofield showed them into what seemed to be a study or office, furnished with a desk, swivel chair, steel filing cabinet and a wall of books and box files. Pictures of Herefordshire bulls and what were obviously thoroughbred horses occupied another wall and a glass cabinet in one corner displayed presentation cups and different coloured rosettes.

The two detectives took it all in at a glance and Schofield nodded again. 'Dad used to breed and show Herefordshires,' he explained unnecessarily, 'and he's been into horses for about three years now.' He hesitated. 'Melanie used to ride too and—' He broke off again, his voice ending in a strangled sob, tears filling his eyes as he tried to maintain masculine control.

Kate's mouth tightened, her chest also contracting painfully as she empathized with his distress. 'We're very sorry for your loss, Mr Schofield,' she said. 'We can't begin to understand how you must be feeling.'

Schofield stared at her for a moment, then nodded but stayed tight-lipped and silent.

Roscoe seized the opportunity. 'You reported your sister missing,' he said, more as a statement than a question.

Schofield took a deep breath, obviously fighting with his emotions. 'She – she hadn't come home by the time Mum and Dad returned from a night out,' he replied, 'and they were climbing the walls when I got back.'

'What time was that?'

'About one in the morning.'

'You were out late?'

'Doing a gig in Taunton – I play bass guitar in a local group.'

'And you reported it straightaway?'

Schofield's face hardened. 'Tried to, but when I rang your headquarters, some dipstick there told me that, as she was eighteen, they couldn't do anything. Force policy or something.'

Kate frowned. 'Just like that?'

'He – he told me to ring again in the morning if she still hadn't come home.' He swallowed hard, choking back more tears. 'And all the time she was lying in the barn like—'

He was unable to complete the sentence and Kate winced. Sometimes police policies were difficult to explain, even if they were made for logical reasons but neither she or Roscoe tried.

'You didn't think of checking the barn yourself?' the DI went on.

Anger smouldered in Schofield's blue eyes. 'Why would I? She hadn't come home, for frig's sake. Why would I think she was in the barn?'

Kate quickly changed the subject. 'And you rang the police again?'

Schofield took another deep breath. 'About 7.30 this morning, yes. The local bobby came out and – and found her.'

'An obvious question,' Kate went on, 'but have you any idea who could have done this awful thing?'

Now Schofield's eyes were really blazing. 'Yeah, I have. Her friggin' boyfriend, Ed Shearing, that's who!'

'What makes you say that?'

He snorted. 'Bastard treated her like dirt. Always playing the field. I told her he was no good but she wouldn't listen and she was out with him again last night.'

'But why would he want to kill her?'

He clenched and unclenched his hands, trembling with emotion. 'Because he's a nutter. Always looking at sick DVDs and he's got a filthy temper. Belted her once. Told him if he did it again, I'd break his legs.'

'But thumping someone is a lot different to killing them.'

He glared at Kate, as if he felt she was trying to defend Shearing. 'Maybe she wouldn't let him have what he wanted, so he took it anyway, then did her in to shut her up.'

'Do you know how she died?' Roscoe put in again.

Schofield nodded, and stared down at his feet. 'I seen her,' he muttered. 'Copper asked me to – to—'

'Identify her?'

'Yeah,' and he shuddered.

'Did you see what she had in her mouth?'

'Yeah, one of them corn dolly things.'

'Do you know where it could've come from?'

Schofield shook his head. 'Never seen it before. They – they sell them in craft shops and places.'

'So I believe. Any idea why someone would put it there or what it's supposed to tell us?'

'How could I? Some sick bastard.'

His voice trailed off and Kate broke the awkward silence which followed. 'Any chance of us seeing your parents, do you think?'

He shook his head and took several deep breaths before he answered. 'Doc's put – put Mum under heavy sedation, so she's in bed asleep, and Dad's, well, conscious but completely out of it. Just – just sitting there staring into space. Even I can't get through to him. You'll have to come back when he's sorted himself out.'

'And when would you suggest?'

Schofield shrugged miserably. 'Maybe never. Doted on her. In his eighties now and it may finish him, I don't know.'

Roscoe nodded. 'I'll have someone give you a call later and see how things are.'

'You do that, Inspector,' Schofield said with renewed vigour as he followed them to the front door, then reached across to open it for them, 'and you'd better get hold of that bastard, Shearing, before I do.'

One foot over the step behind Kate, the DI swung around to face him, his dark boot-button eyes narrowed. 'I suggest you leave things with us, Mr Schofield,' he said, 'or you could find yourself in a lot of trouble.'

'Think I care?' Schofield retorted. 'Someone is going to pay for this.'

And the front door slammed before Roscoe could respond.

'Hot air?' Kate murmured.

'I hope so,' Roscoe replied, 'or we've got even more trouble on our hands.'

CHAPTER 3

THE SCENES OF crime officers turned up in a big white van, bearing the sign 'Scientific Investigations' on the side, half an hour after Kate and Roscoe had arrived and just moments before the appearance of the forensic pathologist.

'Well, she's certainly dead,' Doctor Lydia Summers commented wryly after her preliminary examination of the corpse. 'Not a very pleasant way to go either.'

Roscoe fidgeted impatiently, switching chewing gum from one side of his mouth to the other as the scenes of crime officers in their white overalls moved about in the background like aliens from another world under the direction of the hawk-eyed crime scene manager. 'So what can you tell me, Doc?' he growled. 'Apart from the bleeding obvious, that is?'

Summers laughed, well used to the DI's coarse, truculent manner after years working with the force. 'Time of death, I would suggest, was about midnight—'

'So ten hours ago?' he cut in, looking at his watch.

She nodded. 'More or less, yes but I won't be able to be more definite until the post mortem.'

'At least we won't need a PM for cause of death,' he said drily. 'And the motive looks clear enough to me too.'

Summers nodded. 'Looks like strangulation but not with a ligature. From the bruising, I would say the killer used his hands.' She frowned. 'But there are no *obvious* signs of sexual interference, if that's what you're suggesting, and I won't be able to confirm one way or the other until the PM anyway.'

Roscoe grunted. 'So, if not sexual, what then?'

Summers bent over the corpse again, her mop of tangled grey hair falling out of one side of her protective nylon hood and across her face. 'Sadly, I don't have my crystal ball with me,' she said, 'but it seems to me that a lot more violence was used than was necessary to achieve the death of this poor girl.' She grimaced. 'And the straw doll is a particularly sick feature. It appears to have been inserted with some force and I suspect we will find it has actually ruptured the trachea.'

'Then we could be dealing with a psycho?'

'Very possibly. I'm not a criminal psychologist – but whoever did this would certainly not be someone you would want to take home to your mother anyway.'

'So, a random hit, d'ye think, or something more personal?'

She shrugged. 'Your guess is as good as mine.'

'Hmm. Any other thoughts?'

She smiled sweetly. 'You mean, could I tell you the killer's age, hair colour and inside leg measurement, Ted? Sorry but I've left my Sherlock Holmes detective manual at home with my crystal ball.'

Roscoe scowled but ignored the sarcastic jibe. 'And this PM, when's that likely to be?'

Summers straightened up and turned towards the barn doors. 'Seeing as it's you, Ted, I'll try and slot it in for tomorrow afternoon, OK?'

Roscoe grunted. 'Look forward to it,' he said, matching her sarcasm with some of his own.

Ed Shearing lived with his elderly mother in a neat detached house in Wedmore and was lounging on the settee, barefoot and dressed in just a pair of washed-out blue jeans, when Ted

Roscoe and Kate Lewis were shown into the living room by his mother. The television was on full blast and he hardly seemed to notice their arrival, throwing them just a cursory half-amused glance before returning his gaze to the 44-inch screen and a can of Coca-Cola he was nursing in his lap.

A tall skinny youth in his early twenties – his ribs were so prominent it would have been possible to count them – he had brooding brown eyes, close-cropped black hair and the sort of pointed features and pale spotty complexion that gave Kate cause to wonder what on earth could have attracted Melanie Schofield to him in the first place.

'Police officers, dear,' his mother said. 'Detective Inspector Roscoe and Detective Sergeant Lewis. They want to talk to you.'

Shearing grunted, his gaze remaining fixed on the television, which was showing some sort of discussion programme. 'Do they?' he retorted in a tired drawl. 'Well, maybe I don't want to talk to them?'

He was well spoken, suggesting he had received a first-class education but there was an inbuilt sneer in the tone, which came across as arrogance.

His mother smiled nervously, wringing her hands but did not answer him. 'I'll – I'll leave Edward with you,' she said to Roscoe. 'Er, would you like some tea?'

'Just piss off, will you, woman?' Shearing snapped over one shoulder. 'The plods aren't getting any bloody tea – or anything else for that matter.'

Roscoe scowled, waiting until the elderly lady had withdrawn, closing the door after her. 'Not a very nice way to speak to your mother,' he growled.

Shearing eased himself up into a sitting position and treated the DI to a contemptuous stare. 'What's it to you, Sherlock?' he retorted and belched on the can of coke as he turned his attention back to the television.

Kate watched Roscoe's face darken and winced. Shearing wasn't getting off to a very good start with her boss and that was inadvisable.

'Would you turn the television off for a few moments, Mr Shearing?' Kate said quickly. 'We would like to have a chat with you.'

Shearing looked her up and down and smirked. 'Why should I?' he said without making any move towards the remote on the arm of the settee.

Roscoe stepped forward, grabbed the remote himself and shut the television down. 'Because we say so,' he grated.

Shearing shot up in his seat, his eyes blazing. 'Who the hell do you think you are?' he shouted. 'You can't tell me what I can and cannot do in my own house—'

'This isn't your house – it's your mother's,' the DI cut in, 'and the television stays off, whether you like it or not.'

Shearing jumped to his feet. 'We'll see about that,' he snarled, and turned for the door. 'My uncle is a bloody lawyer.'

The way Roscoe was built, he didn't seem equipped for speed but he moved pretty fast now and Shearing bounced off him as if he had hit a wall, collapsing back on to the settee with a gasp of escaping wind.

Kate turned to look out of the bay window as Roscoe bent over him, one meat-hook gripping his chin and his little boot-button eyes trained on his face like twin pistol muzzles. 'Listen to me, you little shit,' he said. 'I'm not here to play games with you. I haven't the time or the inclination. So you will sit here and answer our questions until we decide we've heard enough. Capisce?'

The Adam's apple was jerking up and down in Shearing's throat as if it was trying to play a tune and his face had grown even paler than before, if that were possible. When Roscoe finally released his chin and straightened up, he sat there staring at him in an obvious state of shock.

'First off,' Roscoe began, 'we did a check on you on our way here and it seems you have quite a bit of form, *Mr* Shearing. Criminal damage, possession of Class A drugs with intent to supply, taking and driving away, assault occasioning actual bodily harm – not a bad list for a twenty-three-year-old ex-public schoolboy, is it?'

Shearing started to say something, his gaze still riveted on Roscoe's face but somehow he couldn't get the words out and he swallowed several times instead.

'And, from what I hear, you also like knocking your girlfriend about?' the DI went on.

Shearing found his tongue and shook his head. 'I never really hit her,' he blurted. 'But she's an air-head. Gets hysterical sometimes and needs to be brought to her senses.' He stared past him at Kate and then back at the DI, his eyes wild. 'Is that why you're here – because she's made a complaint? Listen, she hit me first. That's why I dumped her. It was only a slap anyway—'

'Dumped her?' Kate echoed, turning to face him again.

Shearing nodded quickly. 'She went crazy when I said I wanted to finish with her,' he lied, 'then she just stormed off. What could I do?'

'When was this?'

'About – about eleven last night. We were at a party at my mate's house near where she lives – guy called Josh Turner. It was his birthday bash.'

Kate's eyes hardened. 'You mean you let an eighteen-year-old girl walk home on her own at eleven at night?'

He was immediately on the defensive. 'It – it wasn't that far – just on the other side of the village. Anyway, what was I supposed to do?'

Neither of the two police officers said anything and Shearing went back to his nervous swallowing, his wide-eyed gaze flicking to each of them in turn again. 'Look,' he blurted suddenly, 'what is this? I hardly touched her. If she said I did, then she's lying—'

'She's not in a position to say anything,' Kate said coldly. 'She was murdered last night.'

Shearing sat bolt upright on the settee again. 'Murdered?' he choked. 'You're joking.'

'No joke, Mr Shearing,' Roscoe said. 'Someone killed her last night and we intend finding out who.'

'But when – where? This doesn't make sense.' Shearing gaped as the light of understanding dawned in his eyes. 'Hey, you're not accusing—? Listen, I didn't – you've got to believe me. I mean, why would I?'

He was halfway to his feet again but Roscoe pushed him back down in the settee. 'Maybe you wanted sex and she wouldn't give it to you?' he suggested.

'Or your argument went too far and you lost it – or both?' Kate added. 'Is that what happened, Mr Shearing? She maddened you and you wanted to teach her a lesson but you decided to have a bit of fun with her first – or did that come afterwards?'

'You're sick!' Shearing choked. 'I never touched her. She walked out on me and that was the last time I saw her. It's the truth.'

'What time did you get home?' Roscoe queried.

Shearing looked confused and he ran a hand over his hair, shaking his head and starting to hyperventilate. 'One-thirty, quarter to two, I don't know,' he replied.

'Can your mother vouch for that?'

He shrugged miserably. 'She – she takes sleeping tablets.'

'What about the others at the party?' Kate put in. 'Would they remember when you left?'

He shook his head. 'Unlikely. Most of them were out of their heads by then.' Then there was the sudden spark of hope in his eyes and he snapped his fingers. 'Wait a minute, I remember now. Josh turfed me and his sister out of one of the bedrooms when the party started to break up. Said it was after one and time I was going.'

'And what were you doing in the bedroom?'

Shearing treated her to an unpleasant sneer. 'What do you think? It wasn't sleeping anyway.'

Kate flushed, feeling suddenly naive. 'So while you left your girlfriend to walk home on her own, you were shafting someone else, is that it?'

For a moment Shearing seemed taken aback by her choice of words, then he shrugged. 'Life moves on,' he replied, adding, 'but if you want to confirm it with Josh, his place is called Shenanigans. It's on the main road, just outside the village.'

'Don't worry, Mr Shearing,' Roscoe said. 'We will. Now, can we take a look in your room?'

Kate waited for Shearing to demand to see a warrant but he didn't. Shock had obviously set in, numbing his natural hostility, and he just shrugged. 'My mother'll show you,' he said and he didn't even stare after them as they headed for the door.

Mrs Shearing must have been eavesdropping because she was hovering in the hallway when they went through and she looked more than a little startled when they confronted her. But she recovered quickly and led the way upstairs without even being asked.

The bedroom was at the back of the house and little more than a box room, about seven feet square. It contained a single unmade bed, a chest of drawers and a built-in wardrobe. The walls were plastered with rock and heavy metal posters and the moment they stepped inside the room, a big, black tropical spider studied them from among the debris of a glass aquarium standing on top of the chest of drawers.

Kate knew what Roscoe was looking for and felt sure he would be disappointed. Her assumption proved to be correct. A check of the wardrobe and chest of drawers, after Mrs Shearing had gone back downstairs, produced nothing of consequence, save the usual clothing and some graphic pornographic magazines and DVDs but there were no corn dollies.

'Daniel Schofield was right when he said Shearing was sick,' Kate commented, studying the cover of one of the DVDs with obvious distaste.

Roscoe finished checking under the bed, hauled himself up off his knees and went over to her.

The DVD depicted a naked woman kneeling on the floor of a shadowy room, with a noose around her neck, the other end grasped tightly in the hand of a hooded man wearing a black gown.

'Bondage, eh?' he commented. 'Still, no law against it, is there? Consenting adults and all that?'

Kate snorted. 'Shows the man's a pervert, though, which could be relevant to murder.'

Roscoe shrugged and turned for the door. 'You'd have a job convincing a jury,' he retorted, then grinned suddenly. 'Who's to say what folk get up to on the quiet in their own homes? Maybe even on their honeymoons, eh?'

Kate returned the DVD to the top drawer of the chest of drawers and shut it with a loud bang, glaring at her boss with undisguised hostility but Roscoe's grin was gone almost as soon as it was born.

Shearing was still sitting upright on the settee when they returned to the living room, staring at the carpet. He had lit a cigarette and was trying to smoke the thing, holding it between two trembling fingers.

'We'll be in touch, Mr Shearing,' Roscoe advised, 'but don't go on any long foreign holidays in the meantime, will you? We might want to talk to you again.'

Shearing turned to stare at them. 'So how did she die?' he demanded hoarsely.

'Can't tell you that,' Kate answered.

'But – but where was she found?'

'Can't tell you that either at the moment.'

Shearing scowled at her. 'You bastards can't tell me much at all, can you?' he snarled, some of his courage returning.

'Maybe we wouldn't have had to tell you anything if you had done the proper thing and seen Melanie safely home in the first place,' Roscoe retorted, nodding Kate towards the front door. 'Just think on that.'

CHAPTER 4

THE MAJOR INCIDENT room was still being set up under the direction of an advance party from the Major Crime Investigation Unit when Ted Roscoe and Kate Lewis returned to Highbridge police station and the DI scowled his irritation as he pushed through the double doors into the huge room, then quickly about-turned, narrowly tripping over computer cables on the way out.

'My own office,' he said to Kate out of the corner of his mouth, 'away from this madhouse.'

Kate grinned, following him downstairs to the station's criminal investigation department. Ted Roscoe was old school – an instinct and shoe-leather man – and he would never come to terms with the modern high-tech police service, with its databases, linked computer systems and specialist investigation teams. A good old-fashioned copper, he got results through experience, gut reaction and sheer tenacity and, while he had to work in the brave new world, nothing would convince him to throw in his lot with it.

'So,' he said, pushing out a chair for his favourite DS – though he would never admit it – and dropping into the swivel chair behind his desk, 'what do you think?'

Kate frowned. 'Well, I don't reckon the brother had anything to do with it,' she said. 'His shock was too genuine. And why would he stiff his sister in their own barn? Doesn't make any sense.'

'And the boyfriend?' Roscoe continued, watching her through hooded eyes as he knocked a cigarette out of a packet on the table and lit up.

'Thought you were packing that in, Guv?' she queried, frowning her opposition.

He scowled. 'So did I,' he retorted. 'Now, the boyfriend, what do you reckon?'

Kate shook her head in resignation, then shrugged. 'A nasty bit of work and obviously a weirdo but I don't see him as a killer. He was obviously shocked when he heard what had happened to her. Anyway, he was hardly likely to have driven her home and then attacked her in the family's own barn, was he? Much too risky. He could have carted her off anywhere in his car.'

Roscoe grunted. 'Unless it was a spontaneous thing,' he said. 'Maybe he *did* see her home but just lost it when he tried it on in the barn? We know he's got a violent temper.'

Kate shook her head. 'Feasible but I don't buy it. I didn't like the little toe-rag but I have to say I think he was telling the truth. They had a row at the party – more than likely over the Turner girl – and she stormed out, as he claimed. Then someone else did the business on her.'

Roscoe blew smoke rings, ignoring Kate's look of disgust.

'Someone from the party, do you think? Maybe even this Josh Turner himself? It would have been easy to slip out and back again without being noticed.'

'Unlikely. Why would the killer wait until she got home before making his move? Plenty of places en route for a quick knee-trembler – especially along the lane to her house.'

'Maybe he offered to see her home in the first place? Grabbed the opportunity when she stormed out of the party?'

'Possible but the same argument applies – he would hardly have waited until they got to her house before attacking her. After all, how could he have known whether or not her parents or brother would be there?'

He grunted again. 'We'll need to interview everyone who was at the party in due course anyway – soon as we have the full team up and running. But if that draws a blank, it means we're left with the prospect of a random killer – someone who just happened to be wandering about in the vicinity of her home when she got back – and that is even less likely.'

'Could have been a neighbour returning home at the same time? Sees her, feels a bit fruity and follows her up the driveway?'

'What neighbour? From what I saw of the scene, there aren't any – just a collection of outlying farms, miles apart. We'll have to do house-to-house inquiries, of course but it's unlikely that will turn up anything.'

Kate chewed her lip. 'The corn dolly has to mean something. No one sticks one of those into a stiff's mouth just for the fun of it. There has to be a reason.'

Roscoe stubbed out his cigarette in a tin lid and slipped a fresh piece of chewing gum in his mouth instead. 'OK, so, what sort of a reason? A message? A warning? Witchcraft? Black magic? And why now particularly?'

'Could be someone is trying to put us off the scent. The corn dolly might be just embellishment. But we won't be able to come to any real conclusions about anything until we have a full forensics report on the crime scene examination and Dr Summers has done her stuff at the PM tomorrow.'

'Agreed but we do need to see Melanie Schofield's parents as soon as possible *and* take a look in the girl's bedroom. Should have forced the issue when we were there earlier.'

'They won't be much good to us if they're still out of it.'

'Maybe but it still has to be done.'

'I could try later this afternoon?'

Roscoe nodded. 'That would be good. Before that, though, try and get hold of this Josh Turner bloke. See if he can verify what time Shearing left the party and how long after Melanie Schofield. You'll also need to get a list of the other party-goers. When you've done that, check the internet and also pop into our brand new community library and see if you can do a bit of research on corn dollies. What they mean, who still makes them, where you get them etc., etc.'

'Is that all?' she queried with heavy sarcasm. 'OK if I have a bite to eat somewhere along the way?'

He grinned, sensing her resentment. 'As long as you can fit it in,' he said, then snapped his fingers. 'Oh yes, and don't forget the first team briefing is at 1800 hours. So don't be late.'

Josh Turner lived in a large, expensive-looking modern house on the outskirts of the village and Kate noted, with a touch of envy, the two BMW cars parked alongside each other in the driveway at the side, one silver and one black. Poor little rich kids, she thought sourly and hammered the wrought-iron knocker with a lot more force than was needed. Even so, it was a while before anyone came and when they did, it was a thirty-something man, with blond shoulder-length hair, wrapped none too well in a faded blue dressing gown. For a moment he simply gaped at her across the doorstep, his bleary blood-shot eyes trying to focus on the warrant card held up in front of him.

'Mr Josh Turner?' Kate encouraged.

He emerged from his semi-trance-like state with a lop-sided grin. 'The very same,' he said.

Kate nodded. 'Detective Sergeant Kate Lewis,' she said. 'Highbridge Major Crime Investigation Unit. May I come in?'

His grin faded and he looked puzzled. 'Is there a problem?'

'Hopefully not,' she replied sharply and pushed past him into the hallway.

The reason for Turner's hesitation became apparent as soon as Kate entered the living room. The place looked as though it had been trashed by experts. Bottles, cans and broken glasses lay all over the place and there was a vivid red stain on the fawn carpet that she doubted even the expertise of professional carpet cleaners would be able to remove entirely. Cushions and pillows were strewn everywhere too and, even after the elapse of so many hours, a sweet nauseating smell hung in the air, which she recognized immediately as cannabis.

'Bit of a mess, eh?' Turner grudgingly admitted before Kate could pass an opinion. 'It was a bit of a wild night.'

'So I see,' Kate commented drily. 'Did Ed Shearing ring you?'

She watched the answer flicker in his eyes for a moment.

'Ed?' he echoed. 'Er – yes, he may have done. Can't remember.'

'Don't piss me about, Mr Turner,' she warned. 'This is a murder inquiry, not some Eton College game!'

'He told me what had happened to poor old Mel, yes.'

'And asked you to alibi him, I suppose?'

Turner shook his head vigorously, then winced and held a hand to his head. 'He didn't need to. He was here until at least 1.15 in the morning.' He coughed. 'In my sister's bloody bed. I had to turf him out of it. Wife was pretty upset about it.'

'And where is your wife now?'

He made a face. 'Still in bed. Too much vodka, you know.'

'So what time did Melanie Schofield leave here?'

'Must have been around eleven. Dickens of a bust-up too. She just went for poor old Ed like some she-cat. Had to pull her off him.' He grinned again. 'Highlight of the evening, don't you know.'

'Didn't anyone go with her?'

He made a face. 'Sorry but not as far as I know. We were all pretty plastered by then and Ed had gone back to bed with Sis.'

'And would your sister be able to confirm this?'

'You bet I would,' a husky voice replied from her left and she turned to find a young blonde woman in her twenties standing there. She was barefoot and wearing just a shortie nightie which left very little to the imagination. 'Best lay I've ever had,' she went on and smirked, lighting up a cigarette. 'Poor old Mel never knew what she was missing.'

'And you are?' Kate said tightly.

'I'm Sis,' the girl replied, throwing a critical glance in the direction of her brother. 'Sally Turner.'

'And you live here as well?'

The blonde shook her head and snorted. 'No way. I'm a Cheddar girl. I live up near the Gorge.'

'You do realize Melanie has been murdered, don't you?' Kate grated.

The girl shrugged. 'Tragic,' she said. 'But these things happen, don't they? Part of life and all that.'

'Like the joints you were all smoking, you mean?' Kate snapped back.

Sally Turner stiffened and straightened off the wall she was leaning against. 'I don't know what you're talking about,' she muttered.

'No?' Kate replied. 'Then you won't mind if I have our drug squad take a look around in here?'

'You can't do that!' the brother cut in quickly. 'You haven't got a warrant.'

Kate smiled. 'No but I could easily get one. Then what would the neighbours say?'

Sally Turner glanced at her brother again, then back at Kate. 'We haven't done anything wrong. We just had a party here, that's all.'

'One that ended in the murder of an innocent girl,' Kate reminded her. 'And if I find out later that either of you have been lying to me about what happened, smoking cannabis will be the least of your worries.' She produced her pocket book and a pen. 'Now, I need a list of everyone who was at this so-called party – names, addresses and so forth.'

Josh Turner gaped, then glanced at his sister again. 'Sorry,' he mumbled, 'but – but that would be impossible. It was a sort of open event. There must have been over forty here – didn't know half of 'em.'

Kate nodded. 'Then you can get me the details of the half you *did* know,' she replied, 'and after I've gone, you can sit down with your wife and *Sis* here and try and remember the names of the rest. I'll leave you a card so you can ring the incident room with all the names when you're done.' She gave a thin smile. 'Some strong coffee might help the process. I'll see myself out.'

Kate was still seething about the Turners as she headed back out on to the Levels to re-visit the scene of the murder. What a couple of arseholes, she mused. Totally self-interested and unaffected by the violent death of someone they had once allegedly called a friend. Their attitude just beggared belief. As for the sister, what a brazen little slut. If that pair were representative of the so-called upper middle classes, then God help the rest of society.

Her irritable mood lasted the duration of her short journey and it was not helped by the press reception she received when she arrived at the Schofield house. There were around half a dozen reporters, plus a two-man camera crew, milling about in the driveway entrance – prevented from going any further by bolted iron gates manned by a couple of police community support officers. They were around the car like hornets when she pulled up to the gates and she saw camera bulbs flash repeatedly. Fortunately the PCSOs seemed to recognize her car and opened the gates to wave her in but she almost crushed one of the reporters against the left-hand gate pillar when he tried to squeeze between the pillar and the car as she drove through.

Unsurprisingly, Daniel Schofield was not happy to see her again. His body language made that abundantly clear as he stood in the doorway, blocking her way, and she had to make a supreme effort to put the interview of the Turners behind her and suppress her rising frustration in order to win him over. In the end, however, a combination of tact and feminine persuasion overcame his natural hostility and he reluctantly stepped aside to show her through into the living room, where his mother and father were now sitting.

Ironically, the elderly couple seemed very pleased to see her, despite the situation they had found themselves in, and she formed the impression that their son had been more than a little over-protective. She gained very little from the interview, however. They were both clearly suffering from a considerable degree of trauma, their whispered replies at times no louder than the sound of rustling paper, and, though they did their best to be helpful, they could offer no information about their late daughter that was of any real use to the police inquiry.

She was a good girl. She never stayed out too late. She helped in the house and kept the horses exercised and the stables clean. She was always bright, cheerful and full of life and was liked by everybody who knew her. A perfect virginal teenager, in fact – as most teenage daughters are to their doting parents. There was absolutely no reason why anyone would want to harm her.

Kate didn't enlighten them as to the manner in which she had died and it was plain that Daniel Schofield had so far managed to keep that distressing information from them too. But they were keen to find out – particularly the father – and he pressed her doggedly until his son, for once on Kate's side, extricated her from a very difficult situation, ostensibly to meet her request to see his sister's room.

The bedroom was cool and faintly perfumed, unlike Ed Shearing's, with neat whitewood furniture and a gold-framed bed with a large fluffy toy dog lying on the pillows. Daniel watched, tight-lipped, as Kate went through the chest of drawers and the double wardrobe, clenching his fists when she found the dead girl's diary and started flicking through the pages. But again, there was nothing of interest – just girlie talk about music, fashion and boyfriends. Ed Shearing was mentioned several times, and reference made to his sudden bouts of temper and his wandering eye but overall she seemed quite fond of him and nothing in the diary would have put him anywhere near a dock in the Crown Court. Most important of all, Kate found no trace of any corn dollies, which closed one particular avenue in her thinking, and she left after just half an hour no wiser than when she had first entered the room.

It was raining as she crossed the paved yard to her car and a newly risen breeze set the yellow crime-scene tape still secured across the now-closed doors of the barn fluttering like a twisted yellow and black snake. She stood for a moment, her hand on the door of the car, trying to visualize Melanie Schofield walking up the long driveway on the last fateful night of her life. There was a suggestion of mist in the air again now and she shivered. Was someone waiting for the young girl in the barn or had the killer followed her in there? Why had she gone into the barn in the first place? What had attracted her to it on a gloomy misty night when most girls would have hurried straight indoors? Maybe they would never know but Kate was determined to do her level best to try and find out.

CHAPTER 5

ANOTHER SMALL CROWD was milling about at the front of the police station when Kate got back. Smelling more press, she drove quickly down the side of the building and into the yard at the back but was then forced to sprint through the rear door as a young woman with a microphone in her hand chased after her.

After an hour-long painstaking search on the internet, she came up with a big fat zero. OK, so there was a lot of reference to corn dollies but it was all to do with folklore and European pagan superstitions, and the Somerset Levels never received a mention. It was said that the harvest was believed to make the spirit of the corn homeless, so the hollow shape made from the last sheaf was set aside to provide a winter home for the spirit until the next season, when it was ploughed back into the first furrow in the hope that this would produce a good harvest for the ensuing year. Different customs throughout Britain and Europe were covered and descriptions provided of the various types of corn dolly. But there was nothing to suggest why one might have been forcibly inserted in the mouth of a corpse and in the end, with time running out before the incident room briefing, she gave up and braved the waiting press to try one last avenue.

The new Levels Community Library had been established two years before by a group of local writers, historians and arty types to provide a literary 'window', as they had called it, on all things Somerset – particularly in relation to the Somerset Levels. It was funded by a generous bequest from a well-heeled local philanthropist who had died in a tragic car accident and it had proved to be a very popular alternative to the more traditional public library as a place for specialist research. For Kate, therefore, it was the most obvious first port of call and she reasoned that if the Levels Community Library did not have the information she was seeking, then nowhere would.

The formidable-looking assistant behind the desk was a tall, angular woman of about fifty, with straggly grey hair and pink-framed spectacles on a cord around her neck. She offered no smile of greeting but raised her eyebrows when Kate pushed through the double doors of the imposing building, produced her warrant card and asked her for any information she had on corn dollies.

'Corn dollies?' she said. 'And this is an official police inquiry? Goodness, whatever next?'

Kate chose not to enlighten her, even though she could see that the woman's nose was twitching, and she followed her through to the reference section and nodded a polite dismissal when she was directed to a couple of shelves in a corner dealing with arts and crafts.

She found several books on corn dollies but these covered much the same 'folklore' ground as the internet and then went on to provide helpful hints on how to make the hideous things. Not exactly what she was looking for.

Slipping the books back on the shelf, Kate was about to give up on the whole thing and return to the police station when she spotted an adjoining section on 'Local Folklore' and glimpsed the image of a corn dolly on the spine of one of the books. As it turned out, the book was not predominantly about corn dollies but was a historical account of local superstitions and legends 'of old Somerset'. Curious, she thumbed through it. There was quite a lot about witches, marsh sprites, goblins and hauntings – not really her bag – but there was also a long chapter on corn dollies so, with a rueful smile as she thought of the cold lonely nights she faced at home until Hayden was discharged from hospital, she took the book to the library assistant's desk.

'Sorry,' Pink Glasses said, 'but that section is reference material. Can't be loaned out, I'm afraid.'

Kate grimaced. 'I'm sure you wouldn't want to impede a police inquiry?' she said quietly.

The woman started, her eyes widening behind the thick lenses of her spectacles. 'No, of course not but—'

Kate placed the book on the desk. 'I'll only keep it a couple of days,' she said. 'Then I'll bring it right back.'

The other compressed her lips tightly for a second before giving a reluctant nod. 'Most irregular,' she snapped. 'But I suppose we have no choice.'

She glanced at the title of the book, evidently curious to see what all the fuss was about, and at once her demeanour softened slightly. 'Oh, that's one by Will Fallow – local historian. Lives over in Cocklake village. Often comes in here. Such a nice man.'

Kate nodded. 'Thanks. I'll look after it.'

The woman grunted. 'You'd better,' she said and, making a note of the book, handed it over, adding with heavy sarcasm, 'I hope you enjoy nightmares.'

Kate shrugged, thinking of the current murder inquiry. 'I don't need to read a book to get those,' she replied grimly. 'I spend half my life living them!'

The incident room was already filling up when Kate pushed through the double doors – uniform and plainclothes officers lounging in chairs, sitting on the edges of desks and on window sills, an atmosphere of expectancy hanging the air. Roscoe was already there, standing by a pair of recently erected whiteboards, which carried the first scribbles of the investigation, staring out of the window and obviously waiting until everyone was present and settled before he kicked off with a preliminary briefing. His hands were in his pockets, his head thrust forward like the old bulldog he was and when he turned, apparently sensing Kate's arrival or maybe spotting her reflection in the window, she saw that he was chewing even more furiously than usual.

He beckoned her over. 'So, what have you got for me?'

She made a face. 'Zilch on the research front. Nothing of value on the internet and precious little at the new library.'

He glanced at the book she still held under one arm and evidently read the title on the spine. 'Clutching at straws with that one, aren't you?' he commented.

She gave a short laugh at what was plainly an unintentional pun. 'Or straw *men*, Guv,' she retorted, remembering a reference to scarecrows she had seen in the book. 'Local historian wrote it, apparently.'

'Might be worth asking him about corn dollies then?' he said.

She nodded. 'I intend to.'

He made a wry grimace. 'So, what about Shearing's mate, Turner?'

Her expression hardened. 'Saw him and his sister. Nice couple of beauties,' she replied. 'But they back up his story a hundred per cent, so it looks like he's off the hook. I've got a few names of those attending the party but apparently it was an open-season bash – around forty there – so we're unlikely to pick up many more.'

'And did you manage to re-visit the Schofields?'She nodded and he raised an enquiring eyebrow. 'What did they have to say?'

She shrugged. 'The usual. She was a good girl with no enemies – that sort of thing.'

'Did you check her bedroom?

'Of course but zilch there too. Just a typical teenage girl's room. No corn dollies either.'

He swore under his breath. 'So nothing. I would have liked at least something before the senior investigating officer joins us tomorrow.'

'Tomorrow?'

He nodded. 'Yeah, can't get here before then apparently.'

'Who is it?'

He gave one of his fierce grimaces. 'Believe me, you really don't want to know,' he said.

He followed her with his eyes as she went to join her colleagues now sitting in groups, talking and laughing, at the far end of the room, then cleared his throat and studied them all for a moment. 'OK, you lot,' he barked. 'Listen up and let's get this bloody show on the road.'

Detective Constable Hayden Lewis was lying flat out in the hospital bed in a small private room, with just one pillow under his head, when Kate arrived for a brief evening visit. His hair, which in normal circumstances had been described as looking like an uncut hedge – resembling that of London Mayor, Boris Johnson – was in an even worse state than usual and he had spilt something orange-coloured down the front of his pyjama jacket. Unshaven, with heavy-lidded eyes and a nasty crusted gash on his forehead, Kate thought uncharitably that her new husband looked more like a dosser who had been picked up off the side of the road after an accident than a former public schoolboy and police detective.

'You look like shit,' she commented tightly, dropping a couple of classic car magazines on to the pedestal beside his bed and bending to kiss him on the cheek.

He gave her a lopsided grin. 'Well, *thanks* for that, old girl,' he drawled, 'but why don't you say what you really mean? No point in beating about the bush, is there?'

'The boys and girls send their regards,' she continued, ignoring his sarcasm and pulling up a chair.

'A few guffaws, I suppose?' he said.

She snorted. 'You'd better believe it! Doing your back in on your honeymoon? It will give the wags enough ammunition to last a month.'

He chuckled, then winced. 'Told you I shouldn't have jumped off that blessed wardrobe,' he said.

She didn't even smile. 'So what have the doctors said?' she queried.

He flicked his eyebrows. 'Chipped bone, they think, and maybe a displaced disc but they're waiting for the scan result. Not serious apparently but they want me to rest as much as possible.' He grinned again. 'I've asked for a Swedish masseuse – preferably blonde, about twenty-five.'

'Male, I hope,' she retorted, a wry smile on her face for the first time. 'How long do they expect you to be in here?'

'Couple more days, they reckon. Then it's home to Burtle for a loving wife to take care of me.'

She snorted. 'You'll be lucky. I'm on another murder inquiry – teenager strangled and left half naked in a barn.'

'A barn?'

'Yes. Peculiar job too.' She frowned at him, a sudden thought occurring to her. 'You don't know anything about corn dollies, do you?'

'Corn dollies? Hardly – I played with toy soldiers when I was a lad. Why?'

'One was found rammed halfway down the girl's throat.'

'Kinky!'

'You majored in early modern history at uni, though, didn't you?'

He pursed his lips. 'True but I don't think corn dollies came up much. Mainly kings, queens and lots of battles.'

'Pity.'

'But I do remember that we touched on local superstitions – witchcraft and that sort of thing – and I can recall reading something about dolls being fashioned out of straw and so forth and stuck with pins by witches as a means of stiffing people they didn't particularly like. Might be a connection there?'

Kate looked thoughtful for a moment. 'You could be right. I'll think about that.'

He carefully shifted his position in the bed, wincing at the pain, then forced another grin. 'You haven't been sticking pins in a doll that looks like me, have you?' he said. 'That might explain my present condition.'

She stood up, bent over him and treated him to a long lingering kiss before turning for the door. 'You just pray I don't stick one of those pins in a more crucial spot,' she replied and gave him an extravagant wink as she left.

The little thatched cottage in Burtle village where Kate had lived with Hayden for over two years before their marriage looked less than welcoming when she drove her blue Mazda MX5 on to the gravel driveway running down the side of the house.

For a moment she sat there, listening to the ticking of the hot engine, almost reluctant to leave the warmth of the car and make her way around to the front door through the curls of mist now drifting past the car's windows. Going home to an empty house was never a pleasant experience and, with the gruesome murder of Melanie Schofield vividly etched on her mind, the thought of being on her own for the night had even less appeal.

The teenager's horrific death brought back some unsettling memories of her own too. The two-year hunt for psychopathic killer, 'Twister', following the incineration of two of her colleagues in a police van on a surveillance operation codenamed Firetrap, had become terrifyingly personal. In fact, it had almost cost her her life as well as her sanity and had required a protracted period of therapy before she was deemed fit to return to work. She'd hoped time and her marriage to Hayden – put back several months until she had achieved full recovery – would be the great healer that the quietly spoken psychiatrist had promised but deep down she knew that she would never ever forget her horrific experience and cases like this one served only to bring everything flooding back. OK, so Twister was long since dead but his ghost still seemed to haunt her and even now she felt his cold hand on her shoulder as she finally forced herself out of the car, through the mist to the front door of the cottage.

The open fire was not even aglow now, just a pile of ash – in her present state of mind, reminding her of the contents of a cremation urn – but she didn't bother to clear it out and relight it. She didn't feel that hungry either and, dumping her keys on the kitchen work surface, she settled for egg on toast, an early night and a half-bottle of Shiraz.

It was just dark by the time she climbed into bed and the bed itself felt cold and vast without Hayden to share it with her. She smiled as she thought of the big affable man she had chosen to spend the rest of her life with. Lovable, eccentric Hayden, who never swore or blasphemed and had an almost childlike old-fashioned outlook on life that often made him the butt of jokes by his more streetwise colleagues. Untidy, overweight and so laidback he was practically horizontal, he could be the most irritating man alive but he was loyal, solid and dependable – and, *damn it*, he wasn't lying there beside her!

The rafters cracked above her head as she unscrewed the bottle of Shiraz to pour some wine and she raised her gaze to the shadowed ceiling, cursing her inner fears. Shit, girl, she mused, you're a bloody police officer, for heaven's sake, not some neurotic, off-the-wall head-case. Get a bloody grip! You'll feel a lot better after a good night's sleep.

She probably would have too had it not been for the innocuous-looking library book lying open on her lap. Her main reason for borrowing the thing had been to study the long chapter on corn dollies she had spotted while thumbing through the pages in the library but, as it turned out, the piece told her very little that she hadn't gleaned from other sources already so it was a bit of a let-down. Inevitably, though, she carried on reading and, as a result, was soon drawn into the chilling world of witches, ghosts, ghouls and spectral hounds that Will Fallow seemed to inhabit. The old cottage, with its creaking joints and rustling thatch, provided the perfect atmosphere for such unnerving fantasies, so that sleep soon became the last thing on her mind. As it transpired, that was just as well, for over an hour into the book the 'Legend of Old Strawfoot' stalked out of the dark pages to greet her and ten minutes after wading into the story she suddenly knew she had struck oil. Draining her glass of red wine, she grabbed the phone from beside her bed and swung her legs out from under the sheets as she dialled.

Roscoe had his head buried in a pint of ale at his local when an excited, dishevelled Kate entered the bar and sat down in the chair opposite.

The DI raised an eyebrow. 'Thought you were going for an early night?' he said, glancing at his watch. 'Your phone call sounded urgent.'

'It is,' she replied and dumped the book she had been reading on the little round table in front of him. 'Page sixty,' she said.

He flicked open the cover, his pint pot still raised to his lips with his other hand. 'Drink?' he queried, setting his own glass down while he thumbed back the pages.

She shook her head and he shrugged and settled back in his chair to begin reading.

The tale was only a few pages long and after a quick speed-read he finally closed the covers with a bang and leaned forward in his chair again to study her with a narrowed gaze. 'Strawfoot?' he said drily.

She nodded and leaned across the table towards him. 'It's a local legend,' she explained, keeping her voice low, 'a spectral scarecrow that was supposed to haunt the marshes in the old days and was used by local people at that time to keep the kids in order. You know the sort of thing: "Be good or Strawfoot will get you." Strawfoot was probably the original bogeyman in these parts and he evidently got his name because of the trail of straw he left behind after paying his unfortunate victims a visit. Remember the straw trail we found at the Melanie Schofield crime scene? Strike a chord with you, does it?'

The DI closed his eyes for a second in apparent resignation. 'Please don't tell me you think our killer is a bloody ghost?'

She gave a tight smile. 'Hardly but it's a bit of a coincidence, isn't it? A half-naked girl called Martha Tinney is found strangled in a barn on the Levels exactly 150 years ago. Now the same thing has happened again and the two MOs are almost identical—'

He tapped the book cover with one stubby finger. 'Says here a local gypo, Frederick Laycock, was suspected of her rape and murder, after trying to use the legend to conceal his crime but that he drowned in a peat bog nearby before he could be properly questioned.'

Another nod. 'His mother was a self-styled witch, apparently, and peddled this stuff on a regular basis. He was, by all accounts, a sandwich short of a picnic, so it's logical that he swallowed it all and actually believed he was the bogeyman.'

He lowered his voice. 'But what would be the link between a spectral scarecrow and a corn dolly? Doesn't compute with me.'

'I don't know for certain but if you think about it, a scarecrow's job is to scare birds away from crops, like corn, and the corn dolly was used as a means of promoting a good harvest. That could be the link.'

Roscoe looked unconvinced. 'So, what are you actually saying?'

She tutted her impatience, raising her voice slightly. 'You *know* what I'm saying, Guv. Obviously someone else found out about the legend and decided to run with it. A girl strangled and left half-naked in a barn? It's too much of a coincidence.'

He glanced around him, then said quietly. 'But a 150-year-old copycat killing? Why?'

'How the hell should I know? Maybe our man is a nutter who gets off on this sort of thing.'

Roscoe drained his pint. 'Another bloody psycho?' he muttered, wiping froth off his moustache with the back of his hand. 'That's all we need, because it means this isn't just a one-off; we can expect more.'

He climbed to his feet and headed for the bar. 'Do you want one?' he threw back over his shoulder.

She sighed. 'OK, just a half,' she replied. 'Otherwise I won't sleep at all tonight.'

He grunted. 'I won't sleep now anyway,' he growled.

He returned minutes later with two pints. 'Sorry, I forgot you wanted a half,' he said, his eyes gleaming mischievously at her grimace.

She didn't respond and waited for him to settle himself back into his seat and come out with what was the obvious question. 'OK, so why now?' he queried. 'If your hunch is correct, why would your nutter suddenly start up now? What's got his juices going?'

She shrugged. 'Maybe he's a local man who had a breakdown – just lost it. Or, more likely, he's new here, someone who has moved into our area from some other part of the UK and has adapted his previous tendencies to fit the Strawfoot legend.'

He took a long pull on his pint, then studied her for a moment as she sipped hers. 'At least that would narrow the field down to a few thousand people,' he observed cynically.

'Maybe just a few hundred,' she replied.

He snorted. 'And you think that makes it any easier?'

She didn't say anything and he took a deep breath. 'OK, we'll go with your theory for the time being – but only because we've got nothing else – and your first job is to see the author of this book.' She nodded and he grunted. 'First thing tomorrow. Be interesting to see what he has to say.'

'What about the meeting with the SIO?' she asked.

He grinned. 'Alone in that big empty bed of yours, you'll probably be up, out and back before he even has breakfast,' he said.

She stared at him coldly for a moment, then stood up to go, retrieving her book but leaving her pint glass on the table still half full. 'Thanks for the beer,' she said.

CHAPTER 6

KATE WALKED INTO the incident room the next morning later than she had intended and stopped dead.

The place looked a lot more business-like than before, with a bank of computers on smart workstations, manned by staff she didn't recognize, lining one wall. Printers were set up back to back on a table at one end, plus fax machines, whiteboards and all the other kit essential to the running of an efficient incident room firmly in situ. There was also a television, connected to a DVD player, in one corner and the ubiquitous coffee machine right next to it. Obviously the rest of the MCIU specialists had arrived and everything was on a 'systems go' footing.

An impressive show but Kate had seen it all before and she took in the whole lot with just a single glance, the focus of her attention instead being on the two men standing talking to each other at the far end of the room.

One was instantly recognizable as Roscoe and he seemed to have only recently arrived, since he was still dressed in his overcoat and pork-pie hat, and she knew the other man too, despite the fact that she was only presented with a side view of him. It was a while since she had last seen Detective Superintendent Raymond Ansell but she would have known that thin angular profile anywhere and, without even being told, she knew that he had to be the SIO appointed to run the murder inquiry – which gave her a definite sinking feeling in the pit of her stomach. *Beelzebub*, she mused, recalling one of the nicknames her colleagues had given him when he had been the DCI on the Twister murder inquiry. He was the last thing they needed!

And he seemed to possess some of the Dark One's powers too, sensing her presence as she approached and quickly turning to face her, one hand outstretched. 'Ah, Detective Sergeant Hamblin,' he said. 'It's been a while, has it not? Married, I hear?'

She nodded, reluctantly taking the limp, effeminate hand. 'Yes, sir,' she replied, answering both questions in one go, then adding, 'But the name is Lewis now.'

Ansell tutted. 'Ah yes, silly of me. My apologies, of course.'

'Mr Ansell has been appointed SIO on this inquiry,' Roscoe announced unnecessarily.

Ansell seemed to ignore him, the dark eyes like gimlets in the lean saturnine face as they studied her intently, the slightly lopsided mop of jet black hair, which she had always thought lent him an uncanny resemblance to Adolf Hitler – minus the moustache – drooping forward over the narrow forehead and the smile frozen on the thin lips in an expression that had all the empathy of a stone statue.

In his late forties, with the build of a whippet, Ansell hadn't changed at all in the two years that had elapsed since he had been the DCI and her boss on that last serial murder inquiry – even down to his expensive-looking blue suit and black highly polished shoes – and the aura of cold ruthless efficiency still emanated from him, as it had then, like an invisible force.

'Nightmares all gone now then?' he said in an obvious reference to the trauma she had suffered at the hands of the murderous psychopath they had then been targeting.

She nodded quickly, colouring up. 'It was a long time ago, sir.'

His dark eyes seemed to burn into her and the lips twisted into a grimace that could have been an attempt at broadening his smile. 'It was indeed,' he agreed. 'But memories can – er – linger, can they not?'

She stiffened but said nothing, inwardly furious with him for what she saw as his insinuation that she was still not fit for the job.

Roscoe looked uneasy and tried to turn the conversation away from what he knew to be a very sensitive subject. 'This case is a lot different, though, sir,' he blurted. 'Looks like a plain and simple sex crime to me.'

Ansell turned back to Kate. 'I understand you have a theory of your own, Sergeant?' he encouraged, his eyes now slightly hooded.

She glanced quickly at Roscoe. 'Not actually a theory, sir,' she corrected, 'just a few facts that point in a particular direction.'

Ansell stepped to one side and indicated the door of the SIO's office with a wave of one hand. 'Then let's hear it,' he said. 'But we might as well make ourselves comfortable first.' He smiled at Roscoe. 'I'm sure the DI here can arrange for some coffee to be delivered to us in the meantime, eh?'

Kate couldn't have been more relieved to receive the telephone call from Will Fallow in response to the message she had left on his answerphone. If she was honest with herself, she didn't expect to get much out of the interview she had set up, even though it had to be done. It was more a case of escaping the tense atmosphere of the incident room than anything else. Detective Superintendent Ansell had been in the process of giving her quite a grilling on her so-called theories about the murder when the call had come in and it had got her off the hook right at the critical moment. When she finally got away, however, she was so stressed that she felt almost as if she had been physically violated. Not much team spirit to look forward to on this investigation, she mused as she drove out of the police station yard. Talk about history repeating itself.

Will Fallow lived in a two-bedroom cottage with a tattered thatch and peeling woodwork on the outskirts of the tiny village of Cocklake, and Kate stared curiously at the unkempt patch of garden and the bright yellow Volkswagen Beetle parked just beyond it on a gravel driveway as she walked up to the front door and knocked twice.

The tubby, bespectacled little man with the beaming 'Pickwickian' smile and shabby tweed suit opened up almost immediately, dismissing her proffered warrant card with an airy wave of one hand.

'Come in, come in,' he exclaimed. 'Always pleased to see the police – especially pretty gals like you.' He winked. 'Wife's out shopping in Cheddar, so I can say things like that, can't I?'

Kate smiled at the compliment, wondering how 'Mr Pickwick' would get on with one of her more feminist colleagues. 'I won't tell if you don't,' she replied and followed him inside.

He made straight for what turned out to be his inner sanctum, muttering happily to himself as he preceded her. The room was only about eight foot square but it was made a lot smaller by the crammed bookcases lining two of the walls and the stacks of other books piled on the floor in every available space. A battered oak desk stood against the far wall, facing out of the window, which was cluttered with papers and more books, almost concealing a grey laptop computer and an ancient-looking printer jammed in behind it.

Kate smiled again as she sat down on the swivel chair he indicated and watched him heave himself up with some difficulty and much wheezing on to the edge of his desk, crushing some of his paperwork beneath his ample behind and almost upending the laptop in the process.

'Sorry, Inspector—er—' he said. 'Not used to visitors, you see. Bit of a—um—er—recluse, I suppose you'd call me.'

'It's Detective Sergeant, Mr Fallow,' Kate corrected gently, 'and the name is Lewis, Kate Lewis.'

He beamed again. 'Ah, well, a detective anyway. I feel honoured. What can I do for you?'

Kate hesitated, anxious not to give too much away about the investigation but recognizing that she had to tell him enough to get some answers to the questions she had for him. 'We are currently making inquiries into the death of a young girl,' she said, 'and in connection with those inquiries, I have been carrying out some research into corn dollies.'

His eyes widened. 'Corn dollies? Good Lord, what on earth have they to do with anything?'

'I can't answer that, I'm afraid but my research has led me to read your very interesting book on Somerset's folklore and I was curious about the way a corn dolly featured in the murder of Martha Tinney.'

'Martha Tinney?' he echoed and chuckled. 'Good heavens but that was 150 years ago!'

Kate pressed on, determined not to get side-tracked. 'According to your book, Martha Tinney was found raped and murdered in a barn out on the Levels, with a corn dolly forced into her mouth.'

He nodded, now frowning. 'Very macabre business. But I would correct you on one point. The object in her mouth was certainly described as a straw or corn figure, but it would not have been a corn dolly. Corn dollies were used to bring about a good harvest by appeasing the spirit of the corn. The thing that was left at the scene of Martha Tinney's murder was said by those who found her to have been an evil charm, believed to have been fashioned by a local gypsy and self-styled witch, called Annie Laycock, or Dark Annie, as she was nicknamed—'

'The mother of Martha's suspected killer.'

He nodded soberly. 'Fred Laycock, yes. Bit of a backward youth who was heavily influenced by his mum. Ended up drowning or whatever you would call it in a peat bog, either accidentally or by his own hand – we really don't know which, as the records kept by the local constable at that time don't tell us.'

'You say in your book that he considered himself to be some sort of supernatural spectre, called Strawfoot?'

'Ah, yes, old Strawfoot, the vengeful scarecrow, reputed in the mythology of the Levels to be the entity who punished wayward children. "Behave yourself, boys and girls, or ol' Strawfoot will git yer!"' And he laughed. 'But Fred's paranoia about that was down to his mother. She resurrected the ancient myth – which goes right back to pagan times, long before the 1800s, actually – and used it for her own purposes.'

'And that purpose was to punish Martha Tinney?'

'Sadly, yes. Martha was a rebellious outspoken youngster and well known locally for her promiscuity. When she poked fun at Dark Annie while the old woman was trying to sell her father clothes pegs one day, she overstepped herself and signed her own death warrant. Annie evidently responded by cursing her with the name of Strawfoot but afterwards allegedly got poor Fred to enact the curse by murdering Martha, partially stripping the poor girl to indicate that her promiscuity was the reason for such a severe punishment and leaving the grotesque charm at the scene as Strawfoot's unique sign. Unfortunately Fred exceeded his brief and, before killing the poor girl and leaving her in the obscene state in which she was found, he humiliated her even more by viciously raping her.'

'And what happened to Annie Laycock?'

'They burned her.'

Kate stared at him, feeling the hairs on the back of her neck rise. 'Burned her?'

'Yes. You have to understand that the folk on the Levels at that time were intensely superstitious. When Martha was found and the finger was pointed at Annie by her father, Jeremiah, they actually believed she had employed black magic to call up Strawfoot. They didn't connect simple-minded Fred with the crime, even though the local constable had a more pragmatic view of things. So they took the law into their own hands, hunted Annie down and burned her alive on a pile of straw bales in front of her own cottage.

Then they set about torching every scarecrow they could find in the hope that one would prove to be Strawfoot.'

'How stupid.'

He nodded again. 'Stupid to us, yes but that was 150 ago and things were different then.'

Not so different, Kate mused, thinking of the savage way Melanie Schofield had died.

'But what has all this to do with your current investigation, Sergeant?' the historian asked suddenly, shaking her out of her momentary reverie.

'I'm sorry, Mr Fallow,' she replied, 'but I can't tell you that.'

He nodded again. 'Strangled like poor Martha, was she?' he suggested. 'Partially stripped and left with a straw or corn figure stuffed in her mouth?'

Kate grimaced. 'I'm afraid the circumstances of the case amount to privileged information which I can't share with you, Mr Fallow,' she said firmly. 'And I would be grateful if you would keep our conversation confidential.'

He sighed. 'As you wish but you have to realize I am a historian and, if I may say so, quite a good researcher. I'm certainly no fool, Sergeant, and it doesn't take the intelligence of a brain surgeon to put two and two together with a fair degree of accuracy.'

Kate smiled. She liked Will Fallow. He seemed a nice, genuine man. But she had no intention of confirming or denying things. 'Quite so, Mr Fallow,' she said. 'But one last question. Any idea who still makes these corn figures and where one can get hold of them?'

'Quite a few people still make corn dollies,' he said. 'You know, folksy creative types – sell them sometimes at village hall events or craft fairs – but if it's the sort of talisman or charm that was left at the scene of Martha Tinney's murder, you're talking black magic, witchcraft, that sort of thing, and I know of only one person who might be able to help you there.'

He wriggled himself off the desk, then rummaged through a drawer before producing a dog-eared business card. 'Tamsyn Moorcroft,' he said, handing it to her. 'The Grey Mill, out at Shapwick. Self-confessed witch, actually. She might talk to you, if she's in a good mood, that is but she's a bit of a recluse, just like me.'

Kate took his warm dry hand and shook it. 'Thanks for all your help, Mr Fallow,' she said. 'I'll be in touch if I need to ask you anything else.'

He hesitated, then studied her for a second. 'Just be careful, Sergeant,' he advised. 'Believe it or not, there are some folk in these parts who still believe in the old religion and they may not take too kindly to someone turning over stones, if you get my meaning?' He laughed. 'After all, you don't want old Strawfoot coming after you, do you?'

Kate didn't answer, but in spite of the fragile sunlight licking the weeds of Fallow's unkempt garden as she left, she couldn't repress the shiver that went right through her.

CHAPTER 7

DESPITE THE SUNLIGHT, tendrils of mist twisted and twirled, like delicate strands of white hair, in front of the car's windscreen when Kate pulled away from Will Fallow's cottage and turned left on to the main road, heading back through Wedmore and taking the Mudgley road towards Westhay, out on to the Levels. She made a face as she glanced across the marshy fields on both sides of the road. The mist was never far away in this part of the world and she suspected it would be coming down with a vengeance later that evening. She hated the stuff – it blotted out everything, making driving a total nightmare – so she was determined to get her last job over and done with and shoot back to Highbridge nick as soon as possible.

A few miles further on she reached Westhay village and carried on towards Shapwick, stopping briefly to seek directions from a postman emptying a postbox, before turning off up a rutted track, which cut through fields of scrub slashed by exposed peat and tiny streams.

The track ended after about a quarter of a mile in a large cleared area, ringed by stunted trees and hawthorn bushes with a rhyne to one side. The Grey Mill – a tall three-storey building, faced with wooden slats and in an advanced state of disrepair – stood at the end of the clearing close to a river, its water wheel broken and silent. *Nice*, Kate thought grimly, pulling up alongside an old Mercedes car, laced with rust, a few feet from what was apparently the front door.

For a moment she studied the building, looking for any sign of life but there was none – not even a bird flying over the slate roof – and when she finally climbed out of the car, she was met by a near-total silence, broken only by the gurgle of water from a nearby stream.

There was a rusted iron knocker on the front door but her sharp tap produced no response whatsoever. No one called out with the customary, 'Wait a minute,' no dog barked, no footsteps sounded on creaking floorboards. The place seemed to be totally deserted. She checked the Mercedes next and saw that it was apparently in use; the keys had been left carelessly in the ignition and there were groceries in a couple of supermarket bags on the back seat that someone obviously hadn't had the chance to unload, although the radiator was now cold. So, if the car was in use and still parked there, where was the owner? It wasn't as though they could simply walk out on to a main road and catch a bus or hail a taxi.

She frowned. Maybe Tamsyn Moorcroft just didn't want to answer the door to a stranger? Will Fallow had said she was more or less a recluse and would only speak to her if she was in a good mood. It could be that she'd had a bad day and was even now peering at her visitor from behind one of the curtained windows, determined to stay hidden.

Walking back to the front door, Kate knocked again, then lifted the letterbox and shouted through it. 'Miss Moorcroft, it's the police – Detective Sergeant Lewis. Can I have a word, please?'

She straightened up and stood there for a few moments, waiting but there was still no response or sound of movement inside the place. She frowned again. To come all the way out here for nothing was a pain – especially if the woman she wanted to see was skulking inside. OK, so it was a free country and no one had to answer their door if they didn't want to but Kate was already in an impatient mood and she was not particularly interested in democratic rights.

Acting on impulse, she tried the door latch. It lifted with a soft clunk. She hesitated. 'Anyone here?' she called through the widening gap as the door creaked open. 'Police.'

Silence. She saw that the door opened straight on to a square sitting room, separated from a tiny galley-style kitchen by low-level cupboards surmounted by a wooden work surface, which was littered with unwashed cups and plates. There was a staircase on the right of the sitting area, climbing upwards into darkness and a low arched doorway, to one side of it. Drapes were partially drawn across the windows but, despite the gloom, she could see that the room was furnished with two armchairs, a settee and an oak sideboard, plus an antiquated-looking wood-burning stove equipped with a pipe that rose from the top to a metal plate in the ceiling. There was no carpet on the floor and no television in evidence.

Stepping inside, she looked for a light switch but there wasn't one of those either. The Mill was apparently without mains electricity and, glancing across the room, she now saw a couple of oil lamps hanging on brackets affixed to opposite walls. Gordon Bennett, she mused, talk about living the simple life.

'Hello?' she called again. 'Anyone here?'

Still receiving no response, she crossed to the window and jerked back the drapes to let what sunlight there was into the room. Other features now emerged – glass cabinets, containing a stuffed owl in one corner and a big black raven in another, what appeared to be animal skulls and bones littering the top of the sideboard and a collection of tiny medicine-type bottles on a tray at one end, each containing some form of colourless liquid.

Then she saw something a lot more interesting. Hanging in a line on a piece of cord above the sideboard were four tiny straw-type figures, each with a number of long needles thrust through them and each identical to the corn dolly that had been forced into the mouth of Melanie Schofield

Her heart pounding like an old whistling pump, she swung round and shouted again. 'Tamsyn Moorcroft. This is the police. Show yourself!'

The old building seemed to release a weary sigh but nothing else stirred.

Striding back across the room, she approached the arched doorway, conscious for the first time of a strange unpleasant smell that seemed to be coming from behind the part-closed door. Her skin crawled as she recognized the smell for what it was and, even before she pushed the door right back, she knew why Tamsyn Moorcroft had not responded to her calls.

Like Melanie Schofield, the twenty-something young woman was lying on her back on what appeared to be the floor of some form of stone-walled outhouse or shippon, locks of her shoulder-length blonde hair partially obscuring the upper part of an elfin face. She was naked from the waist down and, also like Melanie Schofield, quite dead, her sightless bulging eyes staring at the beamed ceiling and a small straw figure protruding from between her bloodied lips.

'From the condition of the body, I would say this one's been dead several days at least,' Lydia Summers commented from behind her surgical mask and straightened up from the dead woman. 'As I gather the curtains were drawn when your DS arrived, it's also likely that she was strangled during the night sometime – and, once again, with considerable force. One of her eyes has haemorrhaged quite badly, causing her hair to adhere to the discharged fluid in a couple of places.'

She frowned, indicating with one hand a trail of straw leading from the body to the door. 'All that straw's a bit weird, though,' she said. 'We found the same sort of trail at the Melanie Schofield crime scene, if you remember.' She glanced around the room. 'But, unlike the Schofield barn, there's no reason for any straw to be in here. Really strange.'

'Maybe the killer brought it in on his shoes?' Kate suggested.

'Maybe but there's rather a lot of it for that. It's almost as if it was deliberately left behind.' Summers gave a short laugh. 'Unless we're dealing with a man of straw, as it were?'

Kate shivered. The pathologist obviously had no idea how near the knuckle her unwitting remark was. Before she could think of a suitable reply, however, there was an impatient cough at her elbow. 'But you're saying her death predates Melanie Schofield's murder?' Detective Superintendent Ansell queried sharply, plainly irritated that they were getting off track.

The pathologist nodded. 'Very much so. Your man did this one first.'

'No doubt to silence her,' DI Roscoe growled. 'We found a drawer in the sideboard half full of corn dollies or whatever you like to call the bloody things but only a couple like the ones the killer used. He was obviously a bit particular about design.'

'Well, he would be, Guv, wouldn't he?' Kate put in. 'He's sending us a message and he needs actual straw figures for the purpose – not just fanciful shapes, like the knots and plaited horseshoes that are usually produced.'

Ansell ignored the pathologist's quizzical expression and turned to study her, a half-amused smile on his face. 'So, what *is* his message then, Sergeant?' he said indulgently.

Kate reddened. 'I don't know exactly, sir,' she replied, 'but it's linked to the old murder case of Martha Tinney I briefed you about, I'm sure of it. The straw trail left at both crime scenes also suggests that.'

'Ah, your copycat crime?' he said, his smirk even more noticeable. 'From a hundred and fifty years ago? Taken our man a long time to get underway with it, though, don't you think?'

Kate's mouth snapped shut like a mousetrap. The bastard was patronizing her as if she were some kind of naive schoolgirl. She felt like slapping him across the face but thought better of it. There were easier ways of committing career suicide. 'Just a theory, sir,' she retorted coldly over her shoulder as she turned for the door. 'Maybe someone else will come up with a better one.'

Roscoe joined her outside the mill and, even though it was now dark with the anticipated mist swirling in across the Levels, she knew he was chewing, as usual – she could hear the chomp of his teeth and the suck of his jaws.

'How was the PM then?' she queried, knowing Roscoe and Ansell had attended the grisly event earlier that afternoon.

She heard the bubble from his gum pop as it burst, followed by more chewing. 'Didn't tell us a lot,' he replied. 'Melanie Schofield was manually strangled, as we thought – windpipe crushed – and Doc thinks the straw doll was inserted after death. Interesting thing is there were no signs of sexual interference. In fact, the girl was actually still intact.'

'You mean she was a virgin?'

'Yep.' He emitted a hard laugh. 'Must be unique for this day and age.'

'So why strip her and leave her in that degrading state?' Thinking of Ansell's put-down, she added bitterly, 'Unless it was, exactly as I have suggested, a copycat crime?'

He grunted, declining to comment on her theory one way or the other. 'And why stiff her in the first place? What does the perp get out of it? Knocks my theory about sex being the motive right on the head.'

'Not necessarily. Our man could be a voyeur or someone who gets an erection from the act of killing. He may even be suffering from some form of erectile dysfunction.'

Roscoe emitted a hard chuckle. 'About time you changed the type of books you read, Mrs Lewis – or maybe the company you keep.'

He glanced briefly at the SOCO in her ghostly white overalls going through the back of the Mercedes car under the glare of a pair of spotlights. 'So who was this one then?'

Kate followed the direction of his gaze. 'Tamsyn Moorcroft. Self-confessed witch, according to Will Fallow,' she said. 'These things are apparently not corn dollies but evil talismans or charms associated with witchcraft and black magic—'

'Bad luck tokens?'

'Something like that, yes, I think that is what he was saying – just like the straw figures hanging up in the living room.'

She hesitated, thinking for a minute. 'Thing is, how did the killer know about her? She wouldn't have been someone who advertised in the local newspaper or parish magazine. And what about these straw dollies? He must have researched his subject pretty well to find out about Strawfoot and Martha Tinney.'

'Your man, Will Fallow, would have been ideally situated for that.'

She gave a pointless shake of her head, thinking of the affable little writer with a faint smile. 'He would be the last person I would see as a cold-blooded psycho.'

'But he could have been approached by someone else. Maybe our man did what you did and got hold of his name after dropping in at the local library? Could be where he got his ideas from?'

She nodded slowly. 'You might be right there. I'll check it all out in the morning.'

'You want to run any of this past the boss?'

She snorted. 'No point in running anything past him. He just thinks I'm a neurotic dipstick.'

Roscoe was saved from commenting one way or the other by a sharp voice at his elbow. 'Guv'nor?'

At close quarters, the SOCO who had been checking the car looked even more alien than before, tendrils of mist curling around her like a form of phantasmal ectoplasm and just for a second the carrier bag held up in one hand took on the form of a grinning skull.

'Shopping,' she explained, 'from Tesco.'

'So?' Roscoe queried, turning to face her.

'Got a receipt in the bag,' the woman went on, 'with last Friday's date on it – timed at exactly 7.00 p.m. – 1900 hours.'

'Which suggests she was murdered about five days ago,' Kate summarized, 'probably at some time during the night.'

'Yeah,' Roscoe retorted gloomily, 'so all we have to do now is find out who by!'

CHAPTER 8

HAYDEN WAS LOOKING a lot better when Kate made her second trip to Taunton Hospital to see him after she had gone off duty and freshened up at home. He had shaved and made an attempt at combing his unruly thatch of blond hair and was propped up in bed with an inane grin on his face.

'Not a chipped bone or a fracture, old girl,' he announced confidently. 'Doc says it looks like I slipped a disc and tore some muscles when I went over on that step, so no permanent damage.'

'And when are you being sent home?' Kate queried.

He beamed even more. 'Couple of days still, they reckon,' he said. 'They're going to try a bit of physio first.' He winked. 'Met the physiotherapist today actually – nice strapping girl, lovely blue eyes. Think she'll do me the world of good.'

Kate's eyes gleamed. 'If she does you too much good, you'd better get used to hospital food,' she replied, 'for when I'm through with you, you'll have something a lot more debilitating than a slipped disc to worry about.'

He chuckled and reached over to squeeze her hand. 'Don't tell me you're jealous, old thing?' he said. 'Bad defect, jealousy.' Abruptly, he became serious again. 'How's the old investigation going?'

Her face hardened. 'We've got another stiff – done before the last one apparently. Self-confessed witch, living near Shapwick. Looks like she might have made the straw figure he used on the first girl.'

He frowned. 'Left in the same condition too, was she, then?' he said.

She nodded grimly. 'Partially ingested one of her own creations.'

'Who's the SIO?'

'Guess?'

He raised his eyebrows. 'Not Raymond Ansell? Gordon Bennett, you are the lucky one, aren't you?' He brightened. 'Still, he is a good, experienced detective.'

She snorted. 'Yeah, and a regular clockwork orange too, with about as much charisma as a traffic bollard.'

'Do you want charisma or a detection?'

'A bit of both would be nice.'

He grinned and started to say something but then broke off when a young blonde-haired nurse in her early twenties materialized at his bedside wearing an unbuttoned coat over her uniform. 'My own personal Florence Nightingale,' he said. 'Absolute angel, aren't you, my dear?'

The nurse gave a shy smile. 'It's very good of you to help me out,' she said to Kate. 'I do appreciate it.'

For a moment Kate didn't comprehend and stared at the nurse blankly, while the young woman glanced back at Hayden, shifting her feet uncomfortably.

Hayden coughed, his pale face reddening. 'Ah,' he said, scratching his nose in apparent embarrassment. 'Claire has a bit of a problem, Kate. Meaning to tell you. Her – er – car has packed up and she has no means of getting home. Husband's in security, you see, and away on an overseas contract and she's a bit nervous after the newspaper report about the murder—'

'So you said I would run her home?' Kate finished for him drily.

He beamed again. 'Knew you wouldn't mind, old thing,' he said. 'Claire lives just down the road from us, in Mark village.'

'It *is* OK, isn't it?' the young nurse asked, suddenly looking doubtful.

Kate nodded wearily. Good old Hayden. Feet first again. 'Of course,' she replied. 'But how will you get back here tomorrow?'

'Oh, no problem,' the nurse said with another shy smile. 'I'm four days off after that and can get the car sorted again before I'm back on duty.'

Kate rose to her feet. 'Whenever you're ready then,' she said. 'My car is in the car park.' She treated Hayden to a frosty stare. 'Goodnight, *sweetheart*,' she said, forcing a smile. '*Do* have a good night's sleep, won't you?'

Kate dropped the pretty nurse off at her small bungalow just off Mark Causeway nearly an hour later. The motorway was still packed with rush-hour traffic, delayed by the blanket of dense white mist which had spread across the flat countryside, and it had thickened appreciably since Kate had set out for the hospital. As a result, her journey time had been doubled.

She turned down the nurse's offer of a cup of coffee and waited until she was safely indoors and had switched on the hall light before driving away. Then, tired and still irritable after her frustrating day, she crawled home through the lanes, finally pulling into her driveway with a sense of relief.

She saw the small parcel beside the front doorstep when she dropped her house keys on the path and bent down to retrieve them. Shrugging and wondering who could possibly have sent her a 'present', she picked it up. Then, unlocking the front door with the parcel tucked awkwardly under one arm, she dumped it on the table in the kitchen while she poured herself a glass of red wine from the half-empty bottle on the Welsh dresser.

She had tugged a frying pan out of one of the cupboards and was in the process of slitting open a packet of smoked back bacon from the fridge when the parcel caught her eye again and, hungry as she was, she left the bacon to use the knife on the brown paper wrapping instead.

There was a white oblong-shaped cardboard box inside the wrapping, sealed with tape, and for a moment she hesitated, wondering what on earth it might contain. Like many people, she often received packages from charity organizations, containing raffle tickets, pens and other small gifts to encourage support, and she knew it was always possible Hayden had secretly ordered something nice for her and it had only just arrived. Yet for some reason, she was uneasy. The box was totally plain and looked quite grubby, the tape skew-whiff and wrinkled in places, as if it had been sealed in a hurry. But it was very light, so she reasoned it was unlikely to be anything nasty – like a bomb, she thought, with a grin.

Her grin soon faded when she opened the thing, however, for it contained just one sinister item – the straw figure of a man about six to eight inches high with a note pinned to its chest reading 'Martha Tinney 1846–1863 RIP'.

'So, why you?' Ansell queried, his tone soft but faintly hostile as he stared at the straw doll, still in its box. 'Why not dump this outside the nick here?'

Kate took a deep breath. 'I've no idea, sir,' she said, sensing his antagonism . 'But, as I have said before, there's this book by local author, Will Fallow, about—'

'Oh yes, the legend of—er—Strawfoot?' Ansell cut in, the sneer in his tone very apparent, and he swivelled round slightly to stare at Roscoe. 'Your imaginative copycat theory, eh?'

Kate tensed but bit back the reply forming on her tongue. For a few seconds there was a pregnant silence, broken only by the sound of Roscoe chewing. The tension in the room was palpable.

'Which begs the question, why now?' Ansell continued finally, sensing that nothing else was going to be forthcoming. 'Are we talking about a local resident who has suddenly gone off the rails or some kind of psychopathic misfit who has recently moved into the area and wants a little attention?'

'I've already made that point to Mr Roscoe,' Kate put in, the ice in her tone unmistakable.

Ansell's raised an eyebrow. 'Ah but what have you done about it?'

Kate coloured up. 'Nothing as yet, sir,' she retorted, still smarting from his sarcasm and suddenly forced on to the defensive. 'I've been too busy carrying out the initial inquiries into the first murder. I've already interviewed Melanie Schofield's parents, her boyfriend and the Turners – where the party was held – and I've since been looking into the corn dolly aspect at the new library and through the author of the book I just mentioned.'

Ansell's smile was back. 'A busy little bee, then?' he sniped but before she could say anything else, Roscoe cut in quickly. 'We're doing all we can, Guv,' he said. 'We've already got a team knocking on doors in Melanie Schofield's village, gathering any info they can, and another chasing names from the Turners' party. First light tomorrow, I'll be assigning a further team to cover the area of the new crime scene as well and now you've authorized the installation of Holmes 2, it should be a lot easier to manage the info coming in, and to identify potential links and suspects across the board—'

'We could also get lucky when forensics check the parcel,' Kate added. 'There might be DNA trace elements on the wrapping or the doll.'

Ansell's smile disappeared and he shook his head irritably. 'Unlikely,' he said. 'I suspect this is one killer we will only catch through some good old-fashioned leg work – and there is going to be a lot more of that from now on, Detective Sergeant Lewis, I'm telling you. No more sitting on hands, doing cosy briefings down the pub or visiting patients in hospital—'

'I haven't been visiting just a patient, sir,' Kate protested angrily. 'Hayden is my husband – and I have to abide by hospital visiting times.'

The glitter in Ansell's eyes warned Kate that she was at the end of her length of rope and her mouth clamped shut.

'We are investigating a double murder,' Ansell rasped, thrusting his head forward like a bird of prey in the act of striking, 'and murder investigations don't work around hospital visiting times. We need to get our collective fingers out and nail this bastard before he does another job and the press tear us to pieces. Is that clear enough for you?' He stood up. 'So let's get on with it, shall we?' he continued, without waiting for her to reply, and glanced at his watch. 'Briefing is at ten tomorrow morning, so you should be able to get a good two hours of inquiries in before then, *Sergeant*.'

'Doing what exactly, sir?' Kate said, chancing her arm again.

'What you do best, Sergeant,' Ansell sneered. 'Chasing corn dollies!'

CHAPTER 9

WILL FALLOW TOOK the news of Tamsyn Moorcroft's murder badly when Kate called to see him again the next morning. It was as though the little man had suddenly had all the air knocked out of him in a single blow and he literally fell back into his swivel chair with a gasp, his body doubled up and his chubby jowls quivering. Just outside the study, in the hallway, a grandfather clock reverberated to the Westminster chimes, then struck twelve, although it was still only ten, and through the study window Kate could see an elderly woman – Fallow's wife, presumably – turning over some ground with a fork at the end of a long overgrown garden.

'It's all my fault,' the historian choked. 'If I hadn't told you—'

'Forget it, Mr Fallow,' Kate cut in. 'Tamsyn would already have been dead by then. The killer needed to silence her as soon as he got what he wanted.'

Fallow slowly straightened in the chair, studying her quizzically, as if he only half believed her. Then a sharp gleam stole into his brown eyes. 'So what was it the killer was after?' he queried.

She shrugged. 'We can't say for certain.'

'But the straw talisman being the most likely thing, eh? The one you found in that dead girl's mouth – just like Martha Tinney?'

She grimaced. 'I really can't tell you, Mr Fallow,' she said.

He glanced quickly out of the window at the woman in the garden. 'So why are you here to see me again? It wasn't just to tell me about poor Tamsyn, surely?'

Kate shook her head and, without asking, perched herself on the corner of his desk, as he had done with a lot more difficulty during her previous visit. 'I wanted to follow up on our earlier conversation.'

'But I told you all I knew. What else could I possibly add now?'

Kate's stared at him fixedly. 'You could start by telling me who else you told about Tamsyn Moorcroft,' she said.

Fallow gaped for a moment, then swallowed slowly. 'What makes you think I told anyone else anything?'

Kate took a deep breath, feeling her patience ebbing away. 'The person responsible for the deaths of both women obviously knew a great deal about Martha Tinney and the legend of Strawfoot—'

He made an attempt at a casual shrug but failed dismally and she noted the beads of perspiration on his forehead. 'It was all in my book. Anyone could have read it – you read it yourself.'

'Yes but why would someone suddenly home in on it? Unless they were actually researching local folklore, the average reader probably wouldn't even have been aware of your name or the book.' She hesitated, then added, 'Without wishing to sound rude, you're not exactly famous, are you?'

Surprisingly, he didn't show any sign of hurt or resentment at her candour. 'True but perhaps they *were* carrying out specific research then and came across my book that way?'

'Which narrows down the field somewhat admittedly – but what about Tamsyn Moorcroft? How did they find out about her and her skill at crafting straw dollies? As far as I know, she hadn't written any books and it's unlikely she advertised in the *Yellow Pages*!'

He looked trapped. 'What – what are you suggesting?'

Kate mentally counted to ten. 'Mr Fallow, I haven't got time to play games with you. We have a serial killer on the loose. So who did you tell about Tamsyn Moorcroft, apart from me?'

Silence for a few moments and she saw him squirm in his chair. 'I don't want to get anyone into trouble – I'm sure they're not connected with this terrible business anyway.'

'Who did you tell, Mr Fallow? I shouldn't have to remind you that obstructing a police murder inquiry is a serious offence.'

The colour seemed to drain from his face and he shook his head repeatedly. 'I – I'm not obstructing you. It's just that—'

His voice trailed off but Kate said nothing, simply waited as he appeared to wrestle with his conscience. Then, with a resigned grimace, he suddenly came clean.

'I am president of a local historical society,' he said. 'It's only a small group and we meet once a month.' He hesitated before continuing. 'I – I persuaded Tamsyn to talk to the group about the history of corn dollies at our meeting last month. The talk went well too and she was able to show off some of her creations.'

Kate's heart was beating a lot faster now and she leaned forward to study him intently. 'I want the names and addresses of everyone who was there,' she snapped, a lot sharper than she had intended.

He frowned and for a moment she thought he was going to refuse. But then he released a heavy sigh and nodded. 'We're a very small group of nine and two of our members were unable to attend that night anyway, so there were only seven of us actually present.'

Easing back from his desk, he pulled open the top right-hand drawer and produced a black folder. 'All the names and addresses are listed at the front,' he said. 'But I'll run you off a copy on my printer, if you like?'

Kate flipped open the cover and scanned the list. Four women and five men, including Fallow. 'That would be most helpful,' she said absently. 'So which of them were at the meeting?'

He took the folder from her, detached the relevant page, then swung round in the swivel chair to access the printer beside the desk. 'Says in the minutes,' he replied, raising the lid and placing the page face down on the glass. 'But our treasurer, Jill Rouse, was on holiday in Hong Kong and Neville Haslar was in bed with flu.'

'I'll take a copy of the whole file, if I may?'

'Do I have a choice?' he mumbled and, as he stared into the vivid green light emanating from the machine as it rattled off the page he had just inserted, he had the look of a man who has just committed the ultimate betrayal.

She treated him to a tight smile. 'None whatsoever, Mr Fallow,' she replied. 'But thank you for your cooperation.'

'We've got a witness,' Roscoe announced as Kate dumped Will Fallow's file on the SIO's desk in front of him.

Kate whistled. 'A witness? What sort of witness?'

He scowled at her, plainly unimpressed by the development. 'Some daft mare, a Daphne Herbert, who read that bloody story in the local rag,' he said. 'Just interviewed her.'

Kate frowned. 'So why was she a daft mare? Surely we need any witness we can get hold of?'

'Yeah but there's witnesses and witnesses. This one claimed she saw – and I quote – "a strange-looking man" walking along the main road near Melanie Schofield's place the night she was stiffed.' He shook his head in disgust. 'Said he was dressed like a bloody scarecrow, in a long tattered coat, floppy hat and big boots. Surprised he wasn't also accompanied by the tin man and the bloody lion from *The Wizard of Oz* as well!'

'But maybe she did see someone?'

He snorted. 'Balls! This is what happens when the press start winding things up. We're likely to have every crazy in Somerset and beyond on our backs before long.'

'Even if you thought she was a bit odd,' Kate persisted, 'she still might have seen something, so we shouldn't just discount her.'

He paused in mid chew on a wad of gum. 'Oh, come on! You can't seriously believe crap like that? The woman was round the twist. A ruthless killer stomping around the Levels kitted up in a scarecrow outfit? That's bloody comic-book territory – a *Batman* or *Spiderman* scenario.'

Kate gave another shrug. 'Maybe our man likes to dress the part and is desperate to let people know he is acting out the Strawfoot legend? Could be he is *trying* to scare people witless as part of a sick game.'

Roscoe stared at her for a moment, then shook his head in disbelief. 'You've lost it, Kate,' he said. 'I really think you've lost it. What bloody game?'

'I don't know – yet – but it's worth thinking about.'

He muttered an oath. 'Well, you think about it, Sergeant. I've got more important things to do.'

Abruptly turning his attention to the file from Will Fallow Kate had earlier dumped on the desk, he chewed slowly on his gum as he read.

Kate made no attempt to respond to his put-down; it would have been pointless and she was used to comments like that from him anyway. Instead, she remained perched on the window sill, swinging her legs, while she waited patiently for him to finish his read-through, knowing that, with all his warts, Roscoe was a much more human person to deal with than the acid-tongued Detective Superintendent Ansell who, to her relief, seemed to be engaged elsewhere.

Finally, however, the DI tapped the list of names at the front of the file with one finger and provided his observations. 'So, four women and five men,' he summarized. 'Well, you can wash out the women. Pathologist says the killer was almost certainly male to have had the strength to crush Melanie Schofield's windpipe the way he did and I expect that, when the witch woman's PM has been carried out, we will find she suffered the same sort of damage.'

She nodded but said nothing, and he grimaced his attempt at a smile.

'That's if we're not looking for a butch lesbian with big hands, eh?' he added.

Kate treated him to a disapproving glance. 'Mr Fallow gave me a rundown on the ages of the historical society's members,' she said, without commenting on his tasteless remark, 'and it seems only one of the women is under seventy – and she is fifty-two and confined to a wheelchair. Hardly assassin material!'

He grunted, his moment of politically incorrect humour past. 'So what about our male historians? Done any homework on them yet?'

She nodded. 'One, a Neville Haslar, had just gone down with the flu the night Tamsyn Moorcroft gave her talk, so missed the meeting altogether, and apparently he was confined to bed for over two weeks afterwards, which would have included the night she was murdered. Another, a former chemist named Rex Stavenger, is eighty-one and suffering from chronic angina—'

'Which effectively removes them both from the picture?'

'Yes but the other two – Philip Granger and Maurice Copely – both in their early forties – are worth a look, I think.'

Roscoe brooded over the information for a few moments, then sighed. 'Seems to me we could be stumbling into red-herring territory here. Your historical society could be just a very tenuous long shot?'

She shrugged. 'Maybe it is, Guv but we don't have any short ones at present, do we?'

CHAPTER 10

PHILIP GRANGER WAS a tall, heavily-built local butcher, with big red hands and an equally florid face that pointed to high blood pressure and a liking for both red meat and strong drink. He lived with his pencil-thin wife, Grace – his third partner, as it turned out – in an old detached house with a large garden and outhouses on the edge of Bridgwater. The place was graced by an aggressive-looking black Toyota Land Cruiser parked in the driveway in front of the run-down double garage and when Roscoe and Kate turned up on his doorstep, there was no doubt who wore the trousers.

Brusquely despatching his other half to the kitchen, he showed the two police officers into a small sitting room with paintings and photographs of steam trains adorning three walls. The room smelled of damp and stale tobacco and looked none too clean.

'What's all this about?' he demanded, his high-pitched voice out of sync with his bulk and his pale blue eyes fixed on Kate's open-necked blouse almost hungrily.

Roscoe pushed his chewing gum to the side of his mouth with his tongue and told him.

Granger's thick lips formed into a whistle. 'Tamsyn Moorcroft's dead? Strewth! I read about that other girl, of course but Tamsyn Moorcroft too – it's unbelievable. How did she die? Was it another murder?'

'You met her, we believe,' Kate put in, without answering his question. 'The night she gave a talk to the local historical society?'

Granger nodded. 'Well, not really met her, just listened to some talk she gave on the history of straw dolls or something – bit boring it was too. Trains and cars more my thing, you see. Weird woman, though.' He gave a short laugh. 'Claimed to be a bloody witch – I ask you!'

'So you didn't actually speak to her?'

He chuckled. 'Didn't stay neither. Slipped away during questions at the end.'

'See her at all after that evening, did you?'

He grinned again, apparently missing the significance of the question. 'Wouldn't have minded,' he replied and winked. 'Bit of all right she was – even if she was a witch – but unfortunately never seen her since that night. Sorry she's dead, though. I mean, what a waste. Body like that, eh?'

'Did you know the other girl who died – Melanie Schofield?' Roscoe asked.

He gave an extravagant wink. 'I don't go after teenagers – I prefer mature women.' His gaze returned to Kate's breasts, then he frowned suddenly. 'Hey, what *is* this? Are you accusing me of something?'

'Not at all. Just routine inquiries, Mr Granger,' Kate put in again. 'Nothing to worry about.'

Granger grunted, evidently not entirely satisfied with the explanation. 'Well, I've got things to do today, so unless you've got any other *routine* questions for me. . . ?'

'No, that's about it, thank you,' Roscoe said. 'We'll leave you in peace.'

Kate's face wore a thoughtful expression when she climbed back into the CID car. Granger's surprise about Tamsyn Moorcroft's death had seemed genuine enough but there was a restlessness about the man that she had picked up on immediately and she hadn't liked the way the focus of his gaze had kept returning to her cleavage. In fact, his whole persona had given her the creeps and she was relieved to be back behind the wheel and driving out of the cul-de-sac and away from the old smelly house.

'So,' the DI asked, as Kate drove, 'what do you think?'

She made a face. 'Big powerful man. Probably a bit of a bully, going by his ignorant dismissal of his wife – she seemed a bag of nerves – and from the way he couldn't take his eyes off my boobs probably a bit of a pervert.'

Roscoe chuckled. 'Well, that's succinct anyway – you reckon he fancied you then?'

She shuddered. 'I reckon he'd fancy anything in a skirt – or out of it.'

'So, a probable for us then?'

Kate threw him a doubtful look. 'I don't know. He would certainly be strong enough to overpower any woman but I'm not sure he would have the bottle. More likely to be a fantasist or a flasher.'

'Overall, a bit of a wuzzit then?'

'Something like that. But he did seem genuinely surprised to hear about Tamsyn Moorcroft's death.'

'Yeah but he seemed to know all about Melanie Schofield. Never actually denied he had met her – did you pick that up? Just suggested she wasn't his type. And he knew right away that she was a teenager.'

'So would half of Somerset know that by now, Guv. It's been in all the papers.'

Roscoe gave a reluctant nod. 'Yeah, well – but he didn't look the sort to be a history buff, did he?'

She pursed her lips. 'No but he was obviously a railway anorak and I can imagine him and a couple of other anoraks sitting in a train carriage on the West Somerset line, with cameras primed and corned beef sandwiches on their laps. You couldn't help but notice the pics of old steam trains plastered all over his living-room walls either. Not the most believable profile for a ruthless killer.'

'So why would he be a member of a historical society?'

'Trains have history too. Perhaps he needed an "in" with the historians – or he just wanted the company of like-minded wuzzits?'

Roscoe slipped some fresh gum into his mouth. 'So let's see what the other wuzzit on your list has to offer,' he growled. 'Maybe he collects stamps or butterflies?'

As it turned out, Maurice Copely did neither and the red MGA sports car parked in his driveway suggested he was actually into classic sports cars. He was also a complete opposite to Philip Granger. Tall and thin, with sharp blue eyes and a mop of unruly black hair, his long arms, skinny legs and small head perched on rounded shoulders reminded Kate of a stick insect, although, to his credit, he seemed to have worn well and did not look like a man in his forties. Unlike Granger, his body language was blatantly hostile from the outset, his gaze narrowing and his hands clenching and unclenching as he stared at them from the front door of his modern Woolavington bungalow, even before they had announced who they were.

'Police?' he queried coldly, studying Roscoe's proffered warrant card.

'DI Roscoe and DS Lewis, Major Crime Investigation Unit,' Roscoe responded and out of the corner of her eye Kate saw her boss had noticeably stiffened, perhaps sensing the animosity that confronted them. 'Mr Copely?'

The other nodded. 'So, what do you want?'

Roscoe cleared his throat. 'Could we have a few words with you?' he said. 'It's about the historical society.'

Copely didn't move. 'What about it?'

'Better if we came in to talk,' Kate put in, anticipating an impasse.

Copely hesitated, then shrugged and stepped to one side. 'Not for long, though,' he replied. 'I'm just in from work – early finish today, as I have things to do – and my wife has just put the dinner on.'

The bungalow was bright and cheerful inside and the living room into which the two police officers were shown was nicely decorated and furnished with a couple of armchairs and a three-seat settee. A gold-coloured carriage clock occupied the mantelpiece of a teak fireplace and a photograph of the red MGA sports car stood on top of a bureau in one corner.

For a moment Roscoe and Kate stood in the middle of the room facing Copely, uncertain whether to sit or remain standing, so tense was the atmosphere. The spell was broken by the appearance of a small dark-haired woman with a ready smile and an ample figure.

'Visitors?' she queried.

'Police, Marion,' Copely said sourly. 'Making some inquiries about the historical society.'

His wife laughed. 'Always knew that was a den of iniquity,' she joked, 'but please do sit down. Would you like some tea?'

Roscoe shook his head. 'We'll only be a few minutes, Mrs Copely,' he said.

'Then I'll leave you to it,' she threw over her shoulder as she bustled from the room. 'Dinner to prepare.'

Kate smiled at her departing figure, then settled on to the edge of the settee as Roscoe dropped into one of the armchairs. Copely remained standing for a moment, looking at each of them in turn, then shrugged and sat down carefully in the other chair. But the next moment, to Kate's astonishment, his thin lips twisted into a sneer and he stared directly at the DI and said, 'It's been a long time, Mr Roscoe.'

Roscoe nodded. 'It's just clicked with me who you are,' he growled, 'and it isn't Maurice Copely, is it?'

The other emitted a weak laugh. 'No, I changed my name after all that business – deed poll, you know.'

'Ten years,' Roscoe breathed. 'And now you're here.'

Copely shrugged. 'I have to live somewhere, don't I?'

'And married too?'

'Common law, yes. No bit of paper yet, though Marion has adopted my new name and as far as I am concerned, she is already Mrs Copely.'

'Does your good lady know who you really are?'

A heavy sigh. 'No, and I'd rather she didn't.'

Roscoe nodded slowly. 'So what are you doing these days?'

'Trying to keep out of trouble and working as an assistant at the new Levels Community Library.'

'That can't pay very well?'

Another shrug. 'My father died, left me quite a bundle, so I get by.'

He nodded towards the photograph of the sports car. 'That's how I can afford special toys like that.'

'An old MGA, isn't it?' Kate put in, her passion for sports cars showing through. '1950s model?'

Copely smiled. 'Very good, Sergeant,' he murmured. 'It's 1956, actually. I had it totally restored from a cast-off wreck. Cost me a bomb too.'

The DI glared at Kate, plainly irritated by her interruption. 'So, what got you to join Fallow's historical society?' he went on. 'I would never have seen you as a history buff.'

'Just shows how much you really know about me then, doesn't it? I'm fascinated by it actually.'

'What about straw dolls? They fascinate you too?'

Copely raised an eyebrow. 'Not particularly – especially after Moorcroft's boring talk – why?'

'Funny, Granger said the talk was boring too.'

'Oh, you've seen that fat pig as well, have you?'

'You don't like him then?'

'No one does. He's an arrogant bully. But you haven't said why you're interested in corn dollies?'

Roscoe scowled but didn't answer the question. 'Any idea why we are here?'

'I got a phone call from Will Fallow, so I was rather expecting it.'

'Then you know about Tamsyn Moorcroft?'

'Yes, and to answer the questions you are here to ask, no, I didn't kill her, no, I haven't seen her since she gave us her boring talk at the last meeting and, no, I had nothing to do with the other young woman who was murdered either. Satisfied?'

For a few moments there was a tense silence as Roscoe apparently considered his next question and Copely waited, like a chess player, for his opponent's next move. Kate said nothing. She simply sat there, staring at Copely's face. She felt like an outsider, eavesdropping on a private conversation in which she had no part. It was patently obvious that there was no love lost between Roscoe and this strange awkward-looking man, so their connection had to be something to do with a past case and, although she was dying to know what it was, her instinct was to sit there quietly – watch, listen and await developments – rather than stick her own oar in and be out of sync with whatever Roscoe had in mind.

She didn't have to wait long and it was Copely who kicked off again. Holding both wrists out in front of him, he treated Roscoe to another sneer and said, 'Do you want to cuff me now?'

The DI glowered at him. 'Nothing to nick you for – yet,' he retorted and abruptly stood up. 'But I'm quite sure we'll be back.'

Copely also stood up. 'I'll look forward to it, Detective Inspector,' he said and preceded them to the door, turning briefly as he opened it with one parting shot. 'But next time you speak to me it will be with my solicitor or I'll file a complaint for harassment.'

Kate was conscious of Copely's eyes on them both as she followed the DI down the garden path to the gate but she didn't look back even when she turned to shut the gate behind them. As they drove away, despite her burning curiosity, she made no immediate effort to quiz her boss about the interview that had just taken place and, for his part, he just sat there in silence while she drove, staring straight ahead. Finally, however, she could stand the wait no longer and threw him a quick glance. 'Well, what was all that about, Guv?'

He grunted, lighting up a cigarette and coughing over the first pull. 'Ten years,' he wheezed. 'I was a bloody DS on the NCS, as it was then. And now the bastard turns up again – right out of the blue.'

'So who is he?' she encouraged.

'Our number one suspect,' he replied grimly.

CHAPTER 11

ANSELL WAS BACK in his office when Roscoe stomped into the incident room with Kate in tow and although the cadaverous SIO glanced at them both through the internal office window and beckoned with an impatient gesture, Roscoe did not acknowledge him but made straight for the manager of the Holmes team, leaving Kate to go in on her own.

Ansell gave her a watery smile in greeting and pushed a newspaper across the desk towards her. 'This afternoon's rag, just out,' he purred, 'with a rather illuminating special interest story.'

She glanced at the newspaper and stiffened when she read the headline: 'Ancient Myth Link To Murders.' The story underneath was attributed to a reporter named Bradley Jakes and, after quickly scanning the piece, she emitted a soft whistle. 'I don't believe it. How the hell did he get all this?'

'It seems, Sergeant Lewis,' Ansell drawled, 'that your author, Will Fallow, was duped by Master Jakes – whom he assumed to be a police officer following up on your earlier inquiries. As a result, he gave away a little too much information before he realized his mistake and the paper filled in the blanks themselves. He telephoned the incident room half an hour ago in a panic, after reading the story.'

'Jakes must have followed me to Fallow's house,' Kate grated, then turned quickly as Roscoe burst into the room, blowing a bubble with his gum in a mood of intense agitation.

Ansell barely glanced at him. 'Very likely, Sergeant,' he continued, 'but what I want to know is how Fallow was aware of your theory about the murders being copycat crimes?'

She hesitated, realizing how it looked. 'Well, the man's no fool,' she said. 'He knew I was investigating the two murders and when I asked him about straw dolls and the legend of Strawfoot, he must have put two and two together.'

'Pity we said anything to him at all then, isn't it?' he said, the barbed comment bringing an indignant flush to her cheeks.

'Excuse me, sir,' she snapped back. 'But I could hardly interview him without telling him what I was investigating, could I? And I certainly didn't tell him anything about the case.'

He flicked his eyebrows in silent dismissal. 'Maybe but an irresponsible story like this could cause mass panic. We are likely to be deluged with phone calls from frantic residents startled by bumps in the night or worried about AWOL daughters – which is the last thing we need – especially as there is no sign of a breakthrough in this damned case!'

'I might have something there,' Roscoe cut in before Kate could say anything else. 'Holmes team are on to it as we speak.'

Ansell spread his hands, palms uppermost, in an inviting gesture.

'Blast from the past,' the DI continued, his excitement barely contained. 'Maurice Copely, one of the historical society members, now living in Woolavington. Just interviewed him with Kate.'

'And?'

'Recognized him straightaway. Real name Charles Richard Mottram. Changed to Copely by deed poll apparently. Thing is, ten years ago, when I was a skipper on the old NCS, he was a key suspect in the sexual assault of three teenage girls in the Thames Valley Police area, following a pre con for indecent assault in Surrey. Victims were each snatched over a period of three weeks by a hooded man while walking home after dark. All were stripped naked and touched up but none was actually raped. Theory was, perp had to be sexually inadequate, couldn't get it up—'

'I think sexually inadequate will suffice,' Ansell said drily, glancing at Kate almost apologetically and receiving a sullen stare in return.

'Yeah, well, Mottram's sports car was spotted in the vicinity of two of the crime scenes about the time the girls would have been attacked and fibres found on a Pyracantha bush at one scene matched a torn coat in his wardrobe. I nicked him on sus and he got charged and went to trial–'

'And?'

Roscoe looked uncomfortable. 'He had a good QC,' he retorted defensively. 'Baffled the jury with science – something to do with the forensic evidence being compromised. Anyway, the case was thrown out – grounds of insufficient evidence – and the bastard just walked.'

'Straight to Somerset, it would seem?'

'Yeah, which means he could be our man. Much of the MO in both cases seems to fit.'

Ansell pursed his lips thoughtfully. 'Bit of a coincidence that he is on our patch, I agree but the connection between the cases is a bit tenuous. If Mottram – or Copely as he is now called – *was* the perpetrator in the TVP cases, he didn't actually kill his victims, did he?'

'Maybe he has graduated to that this time?'

'Possible but we have no witnesses and nothing to directly link him with either Schofield or Moorcroft. As for forensics, they've turned up zilch at the first scene – apart from the doll – and we're still waiting on their exam of the second.'

'So we're not going to pull him in for interview?' Roscoe growled.

'On what basis? As far as the judiciary is concerned, he is an innocent man and we have nothing to suggest otherwise. We would be taken to the cleaners if we brought him in solely on the grounds of a past history that had been rubbished in court.'

'So what *do* we do?'

'We watch and we wait.'

'While he stiffs someone else?'

Ansell closed his eyes for a second. 'There may not *be* another incident, Ted,' he said heavily, 'and anyway, you're in danger of allowing your own prejudice towards Copely to cloud your judgement. We don't know for certain that he *is* our man; these murders could be the work of someone personally connected with either or both women – revenge, jealousy, family feud, anything.'

'Maybe one of the teams will come up with a lead at tonight's briefing?' Kate put in, reluctantly burying her resentment against Ansell to avoid letting him see he could get under her skin.

Ansell looked sceptical. 'Always possible but I wouldn't count on it,' he replied. 'No, I think that now the cat is well and truly out of the bag, we should play the news media at their own game and use them to enlist the services of the public. I'll get hold of HQ Press Office and set up a press conference tomorrow afternoon. Maybe a direct appeal for witnesses will get things moving.'

But it was obvious that he had his doubts.

'So why the devil did this weirdo choose you?' Hayden commented, unwittingly echoing Ansell's earlier comments and easing himself up a little higher in the armchair beside his hospital bed with a worried-looking frown. 'I don't like the sound of that at all.'

Well on the mend, although still in a lot of pain, he was desperate to go home but had been told by the hospital that that wouldn't be until the end of the week and only then if the consultant was satisfied his frustrated patient would get the care and rest he needed. That hadn't pleased Hayden one little bit and Kate's bombshell that, while he was incapacitated in hospital, the ruthless killer being hunted by the Major Crime Investigation Unit had left one of his straw dolls outside their home had only served to make him even more agitated.

Kate shrugged. 'Could be it's a compliment – he sees me as a worthy adversary.'

Hayden stared at her. 'Compliment? Are you serious? This fellow is a nutter. You don't want a repeat performance of what happened to you before, do you?'

She chewed her lip, a flashback to Twister momentarily searing her brain like a blinding whiteout. 'I can't do anything about it. I'll just have to be careful.'

He snorted. 'Darned right you will!' He glanced quickly around him and tried to ease up even more in his seat. 'Right, I'm getting out of here. You need me at home.'

She gave a brittle laugh. 'To do what exactly, Sir Galahad? You can't even walk properly. You'd be some kind of bodyguard.'

He slumped back in his seat and winced. 'So what are Ansell and Roscoe doing to ensure your safety then?'

She raised her gaze to the ceiling with a snort of irritation. 'What can they do, Hayd?' she exclaimed. 'I'm a bloody police officer, for goodness' sake. This goes with the territory. Anyway, I don't think our man sees me as a future target – the whole thing is like some sort of a challenge.'

He looked even more worried now. 'Now that *is* creepy. It means he must have developed some sort of fixation about you. You could be in real danger.'

'I am every time I go out on duty. What do you expect me to do – become a nun?'

For the first time since she had arrived he grinned. 'Well, there's a thought. Those sexy black and white habit things are a real turn-on.'

She treated him to a scathing glance as she got up to leave. 'Is that so, Hayd?' she said. 'Remind me when you're discharged and I'll go out and get one for you!'

CHAPTER 12

KATE COULDN'T SLEEP. She had been tossing and turning in the big double bed for at least three hours before she finally gave up. Switching on the bedside light, she slipped from under the sheets and headed for the shower, pausing briefly on the way to peer out of the landing window.

Mist once more choked the Levels, blotting out even the road outside the house, and she wondered whether Strawfoot was out and about at that moment, groping his way through the gloom, looking for another victim.

For some inexplicable reason her disordered brain centred on Mary Shelley, the famous author, who reputedly came up with the idea for her novel, *The Modern Prometheus* – or *Frankenstein* – the night she dreamed of a grotesque face peering at her through the bedroom window of her Lake Geneva hotel. Staring out of her own window now, inevitably Kate found herself half expecting to see a nightmare straw face of her own imagination staring back at her from the mist.

Then, abruptly, she tore her gaze away from the window and continued across the hallway to the bathroom, angry with herself and ashamed of her stupidity for even allowing such thoughts to enter her head. She was actually starting to think of the ruthless killer in terms of some legendary spectre instead of the cold, flesh-and-blood psychopath he really was. She was even thinking of him as Strawfoot!

'Get a grip, girl,' she muttered, 'or it's the funny farm for you, and that's a fact!'

Under the hot jets of the power shower, she soon felt the tension in her muscles begin to fall away as her whole body gradually relaxed and it was with great reluctance that she finally turned the shower off and climbed out of the cubicle, wet and dripping, on to the cold tiled floor. She cleared the steam from the wall mirror and studied her face for a few moments as she dried herself off. She looked tired and drawn, with crow's feet around her heavy-lidded eyes and an anaemic pallor to her complexion, despite the heat she had enjoyed in the shower. Even her auburn hair looked dry and listless when she removed the shower cap.

Her mouth tightened. Surely this damned murder case was not going to make her relapse after so long? The last thing she needed was to end up back on the psychiatrist's couch with a similar lengthy period of intense therapy to that which she had had to endure after the Twister episode. It would finish her career for good. If only good old Hayden was there. His cheerful down-to-earth attitude always did the trick. He was her rock and without him she felt lost and vulnerable.

Finally slipping on a towelling bathrobe, she stomped downstairs in her bare feet and made for the kitchen and the wine rack. The dusty bottle of Australian Shiraz seemed to shout 'pick me' and she smiled wryly as she uncorked it and half filled a large burgundy glass, slopping some of the wine on to the hem of her robe in the process.

Damn it, she was trembling! Taking a very unladylike gulp, she wandered into the living room and dropped on to the settee beside the long-extinct open fire, listening to the familiar creaks and groans of the ancient cottage.

She leaned her head back against the cushion and half closed her eyes in thought, trying to concentrate on what Hayden had said about her vulnerability. What really concerned her was that the killer must have somehow managed to find out where she lived. She never gave out her home address to anyone except personal friends and, as it was ex-directory and also excluded from the public version of the electoral role, the most likely explanation was that he must have followed her home, which meant she could expect to receive a repeat visit from him at any time – a real sobering thought!

She would probably have pondered the issue a lot longer had not extreme tiredness, combined with the effects of the red wine, persuaded her otherwise. As her eyelids started to droop and the wine glass slipped sideways in her grasp, she quickly roused herself, dumped the empty glass on the coffee table and made for the stairs again. It was already after three, according to the clock on the mantelshelf, and it wouldn't be worth going back to bed at all if she didn't make the effort soon.

She heard the crunch of feet on the gravel path outside her front door just as she stepped on to the first riser. She stopped short, staring over her shoulder in the direction of the sound. Silence. Then a faint scuffling noise. She turned slowly to face the door, her heart making familiar squishing noises as the adrenalin began to pump through her veins in a painful head-swimming surge. Someone was creeping about outside the house and it was a damn sight too early for the postman!

Backing across the room to the fireplace, she bent down and picked up the poker. Her bare feet made no sound on the carpeted floor as she approached the front door and peered through the side window. She could just make out the edge of the porch pillar and, despite the mist, it was apparent to her that there was no one there.

Quietly unlocking the front door, she took hold of the handle and paused for a moment, plucking up courage. Then, taking a deep breath, she jerked it open and scanned the doorstep and front garden. Deserted – but there was another small parcel lying on the step up against the other pillar. She was about to bend down to pick it up when she heard more sounds in the mist beyond the faint outline of the garden fence.

'Who's there?' she shouted and, in the heat of the moment, forgetting she was still barefoot, she sprang through the door on to the path, the poker held up in one hand ready to strike. In the gloom to her right, she glimpsed an indistinct silhouette moving away from her at speed. It looked vaguely like a tall man wearing some kind of ragged coat and floppy hat and she froze into immobility as she remembered Roscoe's description of the man Daphne Herbert claimed to have seen. Shit! The old doll had been telling the truth – he was dressed like a bloody scarecrow! Before she could recover, however, the 'apparition' was gone and she was left swearing angrily and hopping from one leg to the other as the sharp gravel bit cruelly into the soles of her bare feet.

Forced to retreat to the doorstep again, she threw another desperate glance into the mist as she leaned against the door frame, sweeping the gravel from the sole of each foot in turn with her hand but there was nothing to see – her intruder had completely disappeared.

Still shaking, she picked up the parcel and went back into the living room, slamming and locking the front door behind her and placing the parcel carefully on the coffee table.

Despite her burning curiosity, she left it there for a moment and crossed to the phone. Business first. Quickly ringing the control room, she called for all available local units to carry out an immediate sweep of the area. Deep down, she was quite sure this would turn out to be futile. Her intruder would be long gone before anyone managed to get there and in the thick mist it was unlikely he would be spotted anyway. But she had to go through the motions or risk criticism later.

Finally turning her attention to the parcel, she studied it for a moment. The thing was about the same size as the little box she had previously received but she made no immediate attempt to open it. By rights, knowing what had happened before, she was duty bound to leave it intact and take it straight to the scenes of crime department in the morning for forensic examination. But at the same time, she was anxious to see what was inside. Another straw doll? Probably but she was desperate to find out for herself.

Chewing her lip, she retrieved the bottle of red wine and, propping herself on the arm of the settee, poured herself another glass, sipping it slowly and studying the parcel through narrowed eyes, as if she expected to hear it suddenly rip itself open like a hatching egg. She was still sitting there, thinking about what to do next, when a car screeched to a halt outside, bringing with it the metallic chatter of a police radio and a powerful flashing light, which sent pulses of blue, like visual heartbeats, across the walls and ceiling of the living room.

There were two of them – a uniformed male sergeant, built like a brick shed, and a thin wiry colleague carrying the 'SC' shoulder insignia of a special constable.

She recognized the skipper as soon as she opened the front door – he was one of the Highbridge team – and she felt his eyes virtually devouring her as she stood there framed by the living-room lights. With a sense of embarrassment, she realized she was unintentionally flashing quite a lot of bare thigh through a gap in her robe and she quickly covered herself.

He grinned. 'No sign of anyone on the road, Kate,' he said. 'Had a good look around the village but you can hardly see a thing in this mist.'

She nodded. 'Thanks, anyway. He probably made off across the fields.'

The uniformed man's eyes sparkled. 'Dressed like a scarecrow, I hear?'

Another nod. 'That's what he looked like – probably a trick of the mist.'

He chuckled. 'Bit early for Guy Fawkes, though, isn't it?' he commented. 'Maybe one of the entries for that scarecrow festival decided to go walkabout?'

She didn't laugh in response and he coughed and shuffled his feet uncomfortably, his grin dying at the same time.

'Want us to – er – come in and take a look around?'

She was conscious of his eyes appraising her again and she shook her head coldly. 'That won't be necessary, thank you.'

He got the message and turned back to the car, almost pushing his gaping colleague out of the way in the process. 'Don't forget to lock your door again, though, will you?'

CHAPTER 13

KATE WAS AT work by nine in the morning, despite lack of sleep, and she attracted several second looks from early-turn colleagues when she passed them in the corridor leading to the scenes of crime office. She had resisted the temptation to open the parcel that had been left on her doorstep and it was still intact when she booked it in with the dour SOCO manager, Samantha Lindslade.

'You look awful,' Lindslade commented, glancing at the parcel on her desk, then studying Kate's pale drawn face with a concerned frown.

'Thanks,' Kate responded. 'But hopefully I'll feel a lot better after you've had a chance of examining that.'

Roscoe was once more in the incident room ahead of her when she pushed through the double doors and he threw her an enquiring look as she walked straight past him into the SIO's office and slumped into a chair.

'Just going to ring you,' he growled, when he joined her a few minutes later with two mugs of coffee.

'You've heard then?' she said, taking one from him with a smile of thanks.

He took a gulp from his mug and studied her over the rim. 'Brief entry in the control room log,' he replied. 'You've had another parcel, it seems?'

She nodded. 'Just booked it in with SOCO – unopened this time, though.'

He grunted and, crossing to the window, peered down into the yard. 'How soon before we get to see what's inside?'

She shrugged. 'As soon as they've finished with it, Samantha Lindslade politely informed me.'

He took another gulp of coffee, then set the mug on the window sill. 'That tells us a lot,' he retorted, then added, 'Guv'nor's on his way to the big house. Briefing with the ACC. Didn't sound too happy when he rang me, so no need to bother him with this just yet.'

'I suspect he'll be a lot less happy once the contents of the parcel are revealed.'

Roscoe faced her, slipping a roll of chewing gum into his mouth and shaking a cigarette out of a packet. 'Yeah,' he agreed, lighting up and tossing the packet on to the desk, 'and he's got a press conference here at 2.30 this afternoon, which isn't likely to improve his mood either.'

He studied her through a cloud of smoke. 'Didn't get much of a look at your late-night visitor, I suppose?'

She shook her head. 'Just a shadow really,' she replied. 'Long tattered coat and some sort of floppy hat, nothing more.'

He started, as if he had been tasered, the cigarette frozen in his mouth. 'You taking the piss?' he gasped.

'No joke, Guv,' she said grimly. 'He was dressed exactly as your Miss Herbert claimed, though I didn't notice much else. The point is, how do we play things now? We can hardly put out a press release to say we're looking for a scarecrow.'

He snatched the cigarette from his mouth and followed the trails of exhaled smoke to the ceiling through half-closed eyes. 'Damned right we can't,' he said savagely, 'and the boss is as likely to put that out at his bloody press conference as he is trying for a spot as a comedian at the Apollo!'

‘So we sit tight and say nothing?’

‘Unless you have any other bright ideas?’

She gave a humourless smile. ‘Fresh out of those at the moment. Did you get anywhere with the check on Mottram?’

He stubbed out his cigarette on the corner of the desk and snorted his disgust. ‘Been a good boy, it seems. Nothing new recorded against him.’

‘So it’s a big fat zero all round?’

‘You can say that again.’

‘Then we can only hope the ten o’clock briefing produces something new,’ she replied, echoing her own misplaced optimism from the day before.

‘Yeah,’ he agreed, ‘but I won’t hold my breath.’

It was a good job he didn’t. The briefing itself, which was left to Roscoe to take in the absence of Ansell, yielded nothing but ‘ifs’ and ‘maybes’ – no forensic evidence, no witness sightings and nothing from the Holmes system – just a few sniggers from the ‘troops’ when the DI passed on the information about the killer’s possible description.

The photographs of Melanie Schofield and Tamsyn Moorcroft affixed to the incident room whiteboard seemed to glare at Kate accusingly as the place emptied of investigators and she stood for several minutes studying the personal details of the possible suspects listed underneath: Daniel Schofield, Ed Shearing, Josh Turner, Will Fallow, Maurice Copely, Philip Granger – the list looked like a pathetic joke. With the exception of Copely and Granger, none of the names really warranted serious consideration but they were the only names they had.

‘So much for the “something new” you were hoping for,’ Roscoe commented gloomily as he peered over her shoulder at the whiteboard. ‘My money is still on that bastard Copely – or Mottram as he was once called – whom we can’t touch.’

‘There’s still the parcel,’ Kate replied. ‘SOCO might get lucky?’

He snorted. ‘Yeah but first I’d have to believe in fairies!’

She turned and gave him a thin smile. ‘Maybe if you did, we’d get that elusive breakthrough we need?’

'I'd be happy to get anything at all, believe me,' he said.

'Be careful what you wish for,' she warned with a short unamused laugh. 'It could be the last thing you want.'

And as if right on cue, the police station tannoy suddenly barked an imperious summons: 'DI Roscoe, contact control room immediately.' At the same moment one of the incident room staff called out sharply, 'Guv!'

Kate felt her stomach sink as Roscoe strode across the room to grab the proffered telephone from the operator, then stiffened before throwing a hard glance in her direction. She was by his side even before he handed the phone back.

'In the car,' he snapped. 'What was it you said about being careful what you wish for? We've got another bloody stiff!'

The young woman was at the far end of the long garden shed, deposits of fresh-looking straw forming a familiar trail between the curled toes of her bare feet and the single door. She was on her back, wearing just a thin yellow nightshirt, which had been pulled up over her breasts, and she had been brutally strangled, her bloodied wide-open eyes registering a by-now familiar expression of terror. Similarly, as with the previous two victims, a straw figure had been forced into her mouth over her projecting swollen tongue.

Kate turned away from the body – trying not to disturb the trail of straw – and stepped out into the cool fresh air, conscious of the perspiration streaming down her face as she removed the protective crime scene booties from her feet. She had guessed the identity of the dead woman the moment Roscoe pulled up in front of the small bungalow a mile or so outside Mark village and she received confirmation of the fact as soon as she laid eyes on the grisly corpse lying in the shed.

'Any idea who she is – was?' Roscoe snapped at the uniformed constable standing to one side of the shed as the DI joined Kate outside.

'Her name's Claire Topping and she's a hospital nurse,' Kate said before the bobby could reply.

Roscoe's eyes narrowed and he drew her to one side, out of earshot of the uniformed policeman. 'Say again?'

'I gave her a lift back here from Taunton two nights ago,' she explained. 'She was Hayden's nurse at the hospital.'

He grunted. 'I learn something new every day,' he said drily. 'Well, you won't be giving her any more lifts and that's a fact.'

She threw him a reproving glance but didn't respond to the insensitive remark. 'What's so worrying, though,' she said, 'is that the night after I run the poor girl home, the killer selects her as his next victim – which suggests that by doing her a favour, I contributed to her death.'

'Balls!' he snorted. 'You can't beat yourself up about that. It's just a coincidence.'

'I don't believe in coincidences,' she replied. 'The killer could have followed me from the hospital that night. After all, he's shown quite a bit of interest in me up until now and must know where I live to be able to leave those damned parcels on my doorstep.'

He shook his head firmly. 'Doesn't add up. What about the other two women? You had no prior connection with them at all, so why should this one be any different?'

'He could have formed some sort of attachment to me.'

He thought about that for a moment, frowning and chewing furiously, then abruptly released his breath in a sharp retort. 'I bloody hope not! The last thing we need is a repeat of the Twister saga.'

She nodded. 'It's worse than that because it also means that, apart from Tamsyn Moorcroft, he must be selecting his victims at random; there's no connection between them or with him personally.'

'Which prompts the question why? If his motive isn't rape, then what the bloody hell is it? OK, so it seems certain he killed Moorcroft to shut her up after getting his hands on her straw dolls but what made him pick Melanie Schofield and this woman here? Both are pretty, in their late teens or early twenties but that's where the similarity ends. One was a brunette, the other was a blonde. Schofield was single and a virgin by all accounts but Topping was married. Schofield lived on an isolated farm, this girl lived in a village bungalow with neighbours each side.'

She shrugged. 'Your guess is as good as mine.'

He treated her to an irritable frown, as if he had been expecting something a bit more positive, then nodded towards the shed. 'And there's all that flaming straw again – same as at the other two murder scenes.'

'*And* at the scene of Martha Tinney's murder, don't forget, so if these murders *are* copycat crimes, as I've always maintained, it figures that our man would want to stick to the original killer's MO as closely as possible.'

'A perfectionist bastard then, is he?' he said and, abruptly turning back to the shed, he glared at the uniformed policeman as if he was the one who had committed the crime. 'How was she found?' he barked.

The other flinched, then cleared his throat nervously. 'Gardener, sir,' he said. 'Arthur Jarvis. Lady apparently employed him to keep the place tidy. Had a key to the shed. Turned up at around eleven this morning to do some pruning and found the shed padlock broken and the lady dead inside.'

Roscoe looked puzzled. 'Found by the gardener?' he echoed. 'Not her husband?'

'Husband's away on a security guard contract with a major oil company in Iraq.'

The DI snorted. 'Pity he wasn't here to guard his wife instead,' he said. 'Where's this bloody gardener now?'

'In – in the kitchen, with my skipper, sir. I was told to stay here until the pathologist and SOCO arrive.'

'At least the plods have done something right for a change,' Roscoe muttered uncharitably to Kate as he led the way to the back door of the bungalow.

The interview of Arthur Jarvis was short and sweet. He was an elderly retired man who did odd jobs for local people for some pin money. He was plainly badly shaken by his discovery and unable to provide any information of any value, apart from the fact that Claire Topping had been a 'very nice lady, liked by everyone'.

'Well, someone obviously didn't like her that much,' Kate said as they checked round the house while waiting for the pathologist and SOCO team to arrive.

'Or maybe that someone liked her too much?' Roscoe retorted. 'But in the wrong way?'

'If the other two women are anything to go by, she won't have been raped, if that's what you're thinking,' Kate replied.

He gave a short grim laugh. 'There are other ways of getting a sexual kick – as you yourself said not so long ago,' he pointed out.

She paused by the half-open French doors and stared at the shards of broken glass on the carpet inside the living room. 'This is how he got in anyway,' she said, ignoring the comment.

He started chewing furiously again and staring around him. 'So maybe he did the job in here?'

She followed his gaze. 'No sign of that. Place looks clean to me – no straw anywhere either.'

As if linked by telepathy, they both left the room and checked the other rooms and very soon afterwards found their 'evidence'. The duvet on the double bed in what appeared to be the main bedroom was hanging over the corner of the mattress, one pillow lying on the floor and the under-sheet badly creased, with clear signs of soiling in places.

'The bastard!' Roscoe breathed. 'He did her in here. But why kill her in the bedroom then go to all the trouble of carrying her out to the shed?'

Kate shrugged. 'Back to what I keep on saying about these being copycat crimes. Just like Martha Tinney, Melanie Schofield was dumped in a barn, Tamsyn Moorcroft ended up in a shippon, which is similar to a barn, and now Claire Topping's corpse is left in a garden shed, which, if you think about it, is the closest thing to a barn he had to hand.' She hesitated, then added, 'But that mattress looks really heavily soiled. Maybe this time he left some traces of himself behind?'

Roscoe considered that for a moment. 'Which could be the very break we've been waiting for. We'd better get out of here and leave it for SOCO to do a proper DNA job.'

In fact, the pathologist turned up fractionally before the SOCO team and Kate was pleased to see it was Doctor Lydia Summers again. It was always good for continuity to have the same pathologist to liaise with in multiple murder investigations – not that she could provide much more than they knew already.

'Well, she's obviously been strangled, like the others,' Summers said, 'and, again, there seems to be no evidence of sexual interference, though, as I said with the previous victims, I'll be able to confirm that one way or the other once I've carried out the PM.'

'Time of death?' Roscoe snapped without preamble.

'I would say around six hours ago.'

'So, midnight, same as before?' Kate summarized.

Summers nodded. 'Same MO all round, it seems. Creature of habit, this character.'

The SOCO van was parked outside the bungalow when they exited into the garden and two members of the team were already pulling on their kit at the roadside.

Samantha Lindslade met them at the front gate. 'Another one then?' she queried.

Roscoe nodded. 'Pathologist is already with the corpse in the shed. Suggest you check the main bedroom first,' he said. 'Looks like blood and soiling on the sheets. Maybe this time we'll get lucky.'

'You already have,' Lindslade replied. 'We've finished with your parcel. Left the contents with your incident room manager.'

'And?' Roscoe encouraged, sensing there was something good to come.

'There are two prints on the tape it was sealed with,' she replied. 'Seems your man has made his first big mistake.'

'Are you running a scan?' Kate put in.

'Already have,' Lindslade replied. 'Did a rush job and called in some favours – especially for you. The marks are sufficient for a preliminary match. They are said to belong to one Charles Richard Mottram.'

Roscoe's eyes seemed to shine. 'Got him!' he exclaimed. 'Bloody Nora, we've got him!'

CHAPTER 14

COPELY WAS STILL at work when the uniformed arrest team descended on his home and his wife stared at the search warrant in astonishment.

'What is all this about?' she exclaimed. 'Maurice is a good man. He hasn't done anything.'

Roscoe nodded brusquely and pushed past her into the hallway, directing the members of the team in various directions, including the shed in the garden. Kate found herself in a small study, just off the hall. It was furnished with a modern desk, a swivel chair and a stand-alone computer, and there were wall-to-wall photographs of otters, herons and other forms of marshland fauna.

'My husband is a keen wildlife photographer,' his wife snapped defensively at her elbow.

Kate nodded absently and concentrated on going through the drawers of the desk. They yielded nothing but more wildlife photographs and *National Geographic* magazines.

'What on earth are you looking for?' Marion Copely persisted.

Before Kate could reply, there was a shout from outside the room and, stepping past Marion Copely into the hall, she saw one of the detectives from the search team talking to Roscoe.

'Found in the garden shed, Guv,' she heard the detective say as she approached and she gaped when she saw that he was holding two straw dolls in his hand.

Even as Roscoe turned towards Kate with a grim smile of satisfaction, there was the roar of a powerful engine directly outside and the next instant the front door burst open and Maurice Copely strode into the hall with fists clenched and eyes blazing from a white mask-like face. 'What the hell's going on here?' he shouted as two uniformed officers stepped forward to restrain him.

Roscoe walked straight up to him. 'You are nicked, mister,' he growled, 'on suspicion of multiple murder.'

The incident room manager made a grimace as he handed over the grotesque object SOCO had left with him in a small plastic tray. Roscoe stared at it for several moments, as if mesmerized.

The straw doll was identical to the others Kate had seen but, going by the album of photographs SOCO had left in the tray beside it, instead of a note, something different had evidently been attached to it originally, although this was now lying on top of the photographs, like a single glittering eye.

'What the hell *is* that?' the DI snapped.

'Looks like a fob watch to me,' Kate replied.

'I can see that but what's its significance?'

'It's the sort of thing nurses wear on their uniforms and Claire Topping was a nurse. He must have taken it from her home.'

The DI's eyes seemed to smoulder. 'And dropped it off at your place straight after stiffing her?'

Kate nodded but said nothing.

'Which means,' he continued, 'that he went to the crime scene fully equipped with all the materials he needed – the box, the tape and wrapping paper as well as the straw doll?'

'Sounds like it.'

'A cool, confident customer then, and one who likes to play games?'

Another nod from Kate. 'That's his Achilles heel – like so many of his kind,' she replied. 'We can only hope that we have actually got him at last.'

Roscoe glared at her. 'What do you mean by that? Don't tell me you have doubts about Copely being our man?'

She looked uncomfortable. 'I don't know – I've just got this funny feeling.'

'What sort of funny feeling?'

She sighed heavily. 'Something in my gut.' She gnawed at her lip for a second, as if reluctant to say what was on her mind, then continued with an apparent careful choice of words. 'Look, the killer so far has been meticulous. He seems to have planned everything well in advance and he has left no trace of himself at any of the crime scenes – not so much as a footprint. It just strikes me as odd that he would make such a fundamental mistake as to leave not just one but two fingerprints on some wrapping tape—'

'Anyone can mess up,' he cut in, 'even the perfect criminal. Maybe he was rushed when he was trying to wrap up the parcel by torchlight or he'd previously handled the tape at home and had forgotten all about it?'

She shrugged. 'You could be right. I just feel uneasy about it, that's all.'

He snorted. 'Don't tell me, it's that woman's intuition thing?'

She smiled faintly. 'Something like that, yes. I'm probably being over cautious. '

'Or just plain neurotic! Listen, it's not often we get a perp so totally banged to rights as this arsehole and the fact that those straw dolls were stashed in his bloody shed suggests to me that he had a couple more victims lined up. At least we might have saved two more innocent lives.'

She sighed. 'I do realize that, but I can't help my feelings.'

He grunted. 'Maybe not but just keep them to yourself when we grill that bastard downstairs, eh? He got away with it once. And I'm going to make damned sure he doesn't do it a second time.'

Yes, Kate thought grimly as she followed him out of the room but perhaps that is the real issue.

The interview room, with its bare bolted-down table and chairs, smelled of stale sweat. Copely had calmed down since being brought back to the police station, but he was still perspiring freely as he dumped himself obediently in the chair next to the hatchet-faced woman solicitor he had asked for. Roscoe settled into a chair beside Kate on the opposite side of the table, flicking on the tape machine. Then he went through the usual pre-interview preliminaries for the benefit of the recording. Copely and his solicitor watched and waited, neither saying anything.

'Right, Mr Mottram,' Roscoe began, 'maybe you'd like to tell us about all these killings?'

'My client's name is now Copely,' the solicitor said for him, 'and he has no knowledge of any killings.'

Roscoe's eyes gleamed. 'Three young women, Mr *Copely*,' he went on. 'Melanie Schofield, Tamsyn Moorcroft and, last night, a nurse named Claire Topping. We know you murdered them, but what we want to know is why?'

'My client denies murdering anyone,' the solicitor intoned again.

Roscoe threw her a daggers look. 'Perhaps Mr *Copely* would like to speak for himself?' he growled.

The solicitor gave a thin smile. 'My client has no comment to make,' she said, 'other than the fact that he has killed no one.'

'OK, so can you explain how two of your fingerprints were found on incriminating material linked to the murder of Claire Topping?' the DI said triumphantly, ignoring the solicitor and staring directly at Copely.

'What material?' the solicitor said.

'A package containing an item of personal property belonging to the deceased was delivered to the – er – police,'

Roscoe replied. 'If you didn't deliver it, Mr Copely, how is that your fingerprints were on some tape sealing the package?'

'My client—' the solicitor began but Copely irritably waved her to silence.

'I've killed no one,' he snarled. 'I haven't delivered any package to anyone and of the three women you mention, I only met Tamsyn Moorcroft once when she was a guest speaker at the historical society's last meeting. This, Mr Roscoe, is a fit-up because you couldn't get a conviction last time. Well, it won't work.'

'How do you explain the two straw dolls found in your shed then?' Kate put in.

Copely's gaze fastened on her and contempt was written into his expression. 'So the little lady does have a tongue in her head then?' he sneered. 'I thought you were just here to hold his hand.'

Kate met his gaze without flinching. 'Why don't you just answer the question?' she said.

'You don't have to answer anything,' the solicitor interrupted again. 'They're on a fishing expedition.'

Copely shrugged. 'I don't mind answering her,' he said and leaned forward across the table towards Kate. 'But I don't suppose you'll believe me, Little Miss Cocksure, when I say I didn't know they were there and that they don't belong to me or my partner.'

'Oh, you mean they were planted?' Roscoe came back in, the sneer in his tone matching the expression on his face.

'Exactly that,' Copely retorted, 'and probably by you or one of your underlings to secure a conviction. Now, are we done? '

Roscoe glared at him. 'No, we're not done,' he replied. 'In fact, we've only just started.'

Copely laughed. 'Oh, you're done, Mr Clever Cop,' he said. 'You said this Claire woman was murdered last night but in your rush to fit me up for the job, you have neglected to ask the most important question of all; in short, where was I last night, between whatever times were relevant?'

'OK, so where were you?' Kate put in again. 'Say, between eleven last night and ten this morning?'

Copely just smiled at her for a few moments, running his tongue along his bottom lip, like a man about to savour a good wine. 'I was in a hide with two other bird-watchers – Janice Young and Neville Haslar – out on the Somerset Levels,' he drawled, 'which you would have discovered for yourself if you had bothered to check my movements before nicking me – I can soon give you their addresses if you want to seek verification.'

Roscoe looked as if he were about to choke. 'You bet we will, mister,' he said. 'But that still doesn't explain how the hell your fingerprints got on to that tape.'

Copely leaned forward across the table again. 'That, Detective Inspector Roscoe, is your job to find out – though after this fiasco and the complaint I intend making, it's possible you won't *have* your job for very much longer!'

CHAPTER 15

JANICE YOUNG WAS in the garden, clearing up fallen leaves, when Kate pushed open her garden gate. Her charming slate-roofed cottage occupied a prime position overlooking the Levels near Meare, with an unobstructed view of the distant blue mound of Glastonbury Tor, and her small front garden was packed with shrubs bordering a neatly manicured lawn.

'A real detective?' she exclaimed with the same sense of awe that Will Fallow had expressed when Kate had introduced herself. 'And a woman too. That must be a bonus!'

Kate smiled, thinking that maybe Detective Superintendent Ansell would have quite a different opinion.

'I write, you know,' Young said as she peeled off her gardening gloves. 'Thrillers mostly. So I am always delighted to meet the police. What can I do for you?'

'It's only a routine matter,' Kate said. 'We just need to eliminate a gentleman from some inquiries we are making – a Mr Copely. I believe you know him?'

She raised both eyebrows. 'What, little old Maurice? What's he done? Nicked a library book?' And she chuckled.

Kate smiled again but didn't accept the implied invitation to elaborate. 'No, nothing like that. Mr Copely says he was with you all last night. Can you confirm that?'

Young chuckled again, waggling a fat finger. 'You make that sound very naughty, Sergeant. But, yes, we are both keen bird-watchers and we spent the night at a hide near the Ham Wall wildlife reserve, trying to spot nocturnal birds of prey.'

'Just the two of you?'

She winked. 'Now, now, Sergeant, whatever are you suggesting?' she mocked, then added, 'Well, initially Neville Haslar was with us, but he came over ill – just got over a bad bout of flu, you see – and had to leave to go home.'

'When was that?'

'Oh, just before midnight, I think.'

'But you stayed on?'

'Yes.' She winked. 'But we stuck to watching birds, I assure you.'

Kate frowned, tiring of the innuendos from someone who was plainly well into middle age. 'Did Mr Copely stay there the whole time or did he leave at any stage?'

'Well, he had to answer calls of nature on occasions but he was only gone for a few minutes.' She became more serious. 'What on earth is all this about?'

'I'm afraid I can't tell you that, but it would be helpful if you could give me a quick written statement.'

She beamed, waving a hand towards the front door. 'But of course, Sergeant, and I might even rustle up some green tea for you.'

Kate winced behind her back. What she had to do for Queen and country, she mused.

Neville Haslar's large country house was set back off the main road in the same village as the Schofields and no green tea was on offer there. In fact, Kate never got inside the place and the reception she received from the tall thin man in the shabby sweater and corduroys was courteous but distinctly cool when he straightened up from the open bonnet of a black Mercedes and turned to face her as she climbed out of her own car in his driveway. The sharp blue eyes studied her with a lazy half-humorous expression from under a rogue lock of blond hair, which had obviously been deliberately combed forward from his thinning collar-length thatch as a desperate denial of his forty-something years. His casual patronizing manner was reminiscent of the arrogant persona of Maurice Copely, although in softer vein, and she gained the impression that he found her visit simply a novel distraction from whatever it was he was doing with his car. But irritating though she found his manner, he was devilishly attractive – she had to admit that.

'Maurice?' he echoed in response to her question and leaned back against the car with the knuckles of his oily gloved hands resting on top of the wing on either side of him. 'What's the silly bugger done now?' He sighed. 'Yes, I was in the hide with him and Janice Young last night, not that we saw much with poor old Janice chattering inanely all the time.'

'I gather you had to leave early, though?' Kate said.

He nodded. 'Yes, I came over poorly around half eleven,' he replied. 'I'd only recently got over a very bad bout of flu, you see. Blessed nuisance. Shouldn't have gone bird-watching at all really. Damned bug still in my system, I suppose.'

'And Mr Copely, was he still there when you left?'

He nodded again, raising one hand to study the oil stain in the palm of the glove, as if he found that more interesting than her presence. 'Don't know how long he stayed, though. Janice is not the most stimulating company.'

'Been a twitcher long?' Kate went on, using the derogatory word deliberately to see how he would react.

He simply smiled again in response. 'Ornithology has been a fascination of mine for over twenty years, Sergeant,' he replied, 'second only to my interest in local history. Member of the local historical society, don't you know?' He winked. '*Wow*, eh?'

'So I believe,' Kate acknowledged. 'And what do you do when you're not twitching or researching local history, Mr Haslar?'

He pursed his lips reflectively. 'I run my own business.'

'Doing what exactly?'

He chuckled. 'Something you would find very boring, I suspect – I provide independent management consultancy to big companies.'

'Why would I find that boring?'

He laughed again. 'Well, it's hardly as exciting as investigating murders, I'll tell you that – and certainly not as fulfilling as my former career in the army. I spend half my time at meetings and focus groups in dusty London offices. That's probably why I became an ornithologist in my spare time – to get out in the fresh air and spend some time learning about the habits of our feathered friends.'

'Is that when you first met Maurice Copely?'

He thought for a second. 'It was actually. Seemed a nice guy, with a bit more breeding and intelligence than the rest of them in the group and a keen – what was it you called me? Oh yes, twitcher, that was it. So we sort of hit it off. Two twitchers twitching together.'

'Do you know much about him?'

He pursed his lips then shook his head. 'Not really. Quiet sort of chap. Works at the local library. Married to a charming lady called Marion. Keeps himself to himself. Keen photographer too and whereas my shed is full of garden tools, his is wall-to-wall photographs.'

'A model citizen then?'

'As much as anyone can be these days, Sergeant. Lives for his birds and his pictures – and he has an equally keen interest in local folklore. Quite knowledgeable on it, in fact. Very impressed with the talk to the historical society by that witch woman, Tamsyn—'

'Moorcroft?'

'That's the one. Said he thought it was really absorbing. Sorry I missed it actually – that was when I first had the flu, you see.'

Kate heard alarm bells jangle in her head. 'But I gained the impression from Mr Copely that he thought the talk was boring?'

He shrugged. 'Not what he told me. Between you and me, I think he took a real fancy to her.'

'Did he make contact with her afterwards?'

'Not as far as I know, though he did say the straw figures she made were exquisite and that his wife might like a couple as ornaments.'

'Did he manage to get her them in the end?'

'No idea. Never asked him.'

Kate pursed her lips and changed tack. 'Did you know the girl in the village who was murdered – Melanie Schofield?'

He shook his head with a disarming smile. ''Fraid not. Bit young for me.' He winked. 'And my wife certainly wouldn't have approved.'

'But this is only a small village and her father is quite a celebrity among the horsey set. Surely you must have rubbed shoulders with him at one time or another?'

'My wife does ride but we tend not to mix with the locals here. Not really our sort.'

'In what way?'

He sighed. 'If you want me to put it bluntly, most of them are not of our class. You know – farmers, labourers, swede types and all that. Different social strata altogether. '

Kate's mouth tightened. 'I see. Bit of a snobbish attitude, if you don't mind my saying?'

He seemed unperturbed by her censure and smiled again. 'Probably but there it is. The old chalk and cheese thing. Damned sorry to hear about the girl's murder, of course.' He frowned now. 'Strangulation is a pretty nasty way to go – saw some of it in the army. This character must be a real nasty swine. But the world is a pretty rotten place at times, isn't it?'

Kate made a face. 'I can't comment on the case, Mr Haslar, I'm afraid.'

But he wasn't about to give up on his questions. 'Press are saying another two women have been murdered too. Do you suspect the same nutter is responsible?'

Kate shook her head. 'Again, I can't comment. All I can tell you is that our inquiries are ongoing.'

His frown deepened to the point of annoyance. 'That's all very well, Sergeant but people hereabouts are scared out of their wits – my wife among them. After all, how can you sleep at night knowing this pervert is on the loose?'

'I do understand, sir,' Kate went on, 'but it's only a question of time before we catch him.'

'And how many more women are going to end up on a slab in the meantime, eh?' he snapped, then almost immediately he gaped at her. 'Just a minute, you don't have poor old Maurice Copely down as a suspect, surely?' He laughed out loud. 'Of *course*, that's why you're here, isn't it? Strewth, I *am* slow off the mark today. But really, the man wouldn't hurt a fly, you must believe that.'

'We're just eliminating people from our inquiries, sir,' Kate replied glibly.

He chuckled. 'I'm sure you are – me too, I expect?'

Kate sensed the implied question and gave a brief smile. 'Thank you for your time, Mr Haslar,' she said. 'Can I just get a quick written statement off you before I leave?'

'Be delighted, Detective Sergeant,' he said, throwing open a rear passenger door of his car. 'And, if you write it for me, I'll even let you use my Merc as your office – I take it you *do* have a pen?'

Detective Superintendent Ansell was less than impressed with the day's events when he returned to the incident room and under his gaze DI Roscoe fidgeted on his chair like a naughty boy.

'I assume you have checked out Copely's alibi?' Ansell drawled, his dark eyes hard and critical.

Roscoe pushed his chewing gum to the side of his mouth and nodded. 'Kate's interviewed both the so-called twitchers – a Janice Young and a Neville Haslar,' he said. 'Both confirm Copely was with them at the hide when he claimed, although Haslar was only there the early part of the night and had to leave just before midnight because of a recurring illness.'

Ansell considered the information for a moment and shrugged. 'Not entirely conclusive then, but corroborative enough from Copely's point of view to let him off the hook for the time being. Are we sure the fingerprint evidence was accurate?'

'Yes, sir,' Kate said. 'SOCO have double-checked and the prints do belong to our man.'

Ansell sighed. 'So how did his dabs end up on the package? That is what we should be asking ourselves. Anything special about the tape or the wrappings?'

Kate shook her head. 'Ordinary Sellotape and brown paper that you can get from any stationers and the box was a standard plain cardboard thing that could have come from anywhere – just like the last one.'

Ansell leaned back in his chair, his fingertips together. 'So we are faced with something of a conundrum,' he said, adding, 'and, from what you have told me, the disturbing revelation that our killer likes to wander about dressed as a scarecrow?'

Kate couldn't resist a quick 'told you so' dig. 'Looks like I was right about the copycat thing all along then, sir, doesn't it?' she said.

Ansell's eyes narrowed and his cobra-like gaze fastened on her face. 'So it would seem, Sergeant,' he said softly. 'So all you have to do now is to get me a result – like yesterday!'

CHAPTER 16

THE NAKED BODY of the young nurse had the appearance of a gutted animal lying on its back on the stainless steel dissecting table and Kate shuddered as the scalp, with its mass of blonde hair, was deftly pulled back over the top of the skull, which had been sliced off earlier to allow the brain to be removed and examined and then replaced like some kind of obscene lid. The mortuary assistant engaged in the gruesome task then turned his attention to the trunk of the body and the horrendous incision in the torso, running from the breast bone right down to the lower abdomen. The internal organs, mutilated by the pathologist's knife during examination, had already been returned to the cavity and he now began the task of crudely sewing up the incision, humming quietly to himself like a man innocently stitching up a turkey for a Christmas dinner.

The photographer was already packing up his equipment when she entered the mortuary with Roscoe, and Doctor Summers glanced briefly at them over her shoulder as she washed her surgical gloves off under a tap before dumping them into the clinical waste-bin.

'Sorry to put you through this, Kate,' Roscoe muttered. 'I had to call you over as the guv'nor's tied up with some damned press editor and it's necessary to corroborate everything in cases like this.'

Kate looked distinctly affronted. 'I'm a copper and a bloody DS, Guv,' she snapped, 'not some shrinking violet. Don't you think I've been to post mortems before?'

He gave an apologetic grin. 'Sorry,' he said again. 'I didn't mean . . . It's just that—'

'I'm a woman?' Kate finished for him, her anger growing. 'And so is the pathologist, if I'm not mistaken, so please don't patronize me!'

He winced and seemed grateful when Lydia Summers rescued him from the hole he had dug for himself with a cheerful, 'Afternoon, people. Just finished.'

'So what can you tell us?' Roscoe said quickly, treating Kate to a brief sideways glance.

Summers shrugged. 'Well, she didn't die of old age, that's for sure,' she said with a grin. 'From the condition of the body, I'd reaffirm what I said yesterday that time of death was close to midnight. Same MO as the other two women – but you know that already, don't you? Oh yes, and there are no signs of rape or any sexual interference. In fact, although she's plainly not a virgin, there are no signs of recent intercourse either.'

'Bit difficult when her husband is in Iraq,' Roscoe commented drily.

'Not if she was over the side,' Kate commented, her tone still hostile.

Summers shrugged. 'Well, the indications are that she's been a good girl in the twenty-four hours prior to her death anyway.'

'So rape was obviously not the motive in respect of any of the victims,' Roscoe summarized. 'What about the soiled bedclothes? Her fluids or someone else's?'

Summers pursed her lips. 'Difficult to say until the results come back from the lab, but I'd hazard a guess that they were the consequence of sudden violent death. We found similar traces under the bodies at the other two crime scenes. Quite common in such cases actually.'

'So no chance of a DNA match with the killer then?'

The pathologist frowned. 'Unlikely, I'd say but I thought you'd already arrested someone?'

Roscoe cleared his throat. 'Looks like a blind alley,' he said without elaborating on the issue. 'Back to square one.'

Summers nodded. 'In that case, I might be able to throw a little more light on things for you.'

'I'm all ears.'

She walked to the head of the corpse and, bending down, pointed at the base of the neck. 'See there?'

Kate got there first and Roscoe peered over her shoulder. At once she saw the bruises – small irregular patches on both sides of the neck.

'Compression marks,' Summers explained. 'That have become more pronounced with time and they were evident on all three corpses when I checked.'

'How come no one noticed these before?' Kate queried.

'They did and your SOCO took pics of them but compression marks are a common feature of strangulation cases and they take time to come out fully, so they were just accepted as the norm – as they were with the other two victims.'

'What makes them significant in this case then?' Roscoe asked.

Summers pointed at the marks again. 'Look more closely. What do you see?'

Roscoe made a face. 'What are we supposed to see? Three marks at the back of the neck, two more at the front.'

Summers' eyes gleamed. 'Think again. The human hand has five digits or metacarpal bones and fourteen phalanges or phalanx bones. Each of the four fingers has three phalanx bones, a distal – which carries the fingernail – an intermediate and a proximal phalanx, while the thumb has just two, with no intermediate phalanx. To put it simply – there is a thumb, an index finger, middle finger, ring finger and what is commonly called the pinky or little finger. With me so far?'

'Just get on with it,' Roscoe growled.' We haven't got time for a lesson in anatomy.'

'In a strangulation, the thumbs obviously do the main damage,' Summers continued, apparently enjoying herself, 'with the other fingers supporting them in a powerful grip around the throat, compressing the trachea. Of those, the little finger does the least, but the other three fingers with their extended distal phalanges enable compression to be fatally exerted—'

Kate cut in before she could finish her explanation. 'I get it!' she exclaimed. 'Excluding the deep bruises from the thumbs on the throat, there are three main marks on the right side of her neck but only two on the left.'

Summers positively beamed, like a schoolteacher whose pupil has finally sussed the answer to a key question. 'Exactly,' she replied. 'And this killer exerted considerably more pressure than was necessary.'

'Meaning what?' Roscoe snapped. 'We seem to be playing games here.'

'No games, Ted,' Summers contradicted.

'He's missing a finger,' Kate breathed. 'Three pressure marks on one side and four on the other suggest that he only has three fingers on his left hand, including the little finger.'

'With the ring finger being the missing one,' Summers finished. 'And those fingers will be long and powerful, going by the position of the marks well towards the back of the neck, resulting in the fracture of the hyoid bone and thyroid cartilage.'

Instead of looking pleased at the pathologist's findings, Roscoe's expression darkened. 'That rules out Copely completely then,' he said gloomily.

Kate stared at him in astonishment. 'Maybe it does,' she agreed, 'but it certainly rules someone else *in*! All we've got to do is to find him.'

'So a picture is at last starting to emerge then,' Ansell commented when Roscoe and Kate reported back. 'Still a bit hazy but gradually firming up.'

Kate nodded, frowning when she saw that Roscoe still wore his gloomy, disappointed expression. 'We now know we are looking for a powerfully built man with the ring finger missing from his left hand,' she said. 'which brings us a step closer to nailing our man, if we manage to identify a suspect.'

Roscoe still seemed unenthused. 'If is a very big word, Kate,' he said. 'At present we don't *have* any suspects, and if this character's got no form, a descriptive index search won't turn up anything, so we'd still be up shit creek without a paddle.'

'Nice to see you are still in a positive frame of mind, Ted,' Ansell said with heavy sarcasm. 'So what other helpful suggestions have you to share with us?'

Roscoe gave a sheepish grin. 'Sorry, Guv,' he replied. 'Getting old and jaded, that's all. It's just that we seem to be walking in treacle on this one and I really thought the fingerprints on that tape would clinch things.'

Ansell nodded. 'Part of the puzzle we have yet to solve,' he said. 'At the very least it could suggest the killer either associates or works with Copely – perhaps Copely borrowed the tape from him at some stage to wrap something up in or repair it?'

'Bit of a wild card, that, Guv,' Roscoe argued. 'Equally, Copely could have picked the tape up in a stationery shop, such as WH Smiths but decided against buying it, leaving the killer to buy it at a later date instead.'

'So why is the rest of the tape clean of prints?' Ansell persisted. 'By all accounts, you would have expected other customers to have handled it as well.'

'The library,' Kate breathed. 'Why the hell didn't I think of that before?'

Ansell directed an interrogative glance in her direction. 'Perhaps you'd like to share that particular pearl of wisdom with us, Sergeant?' he drawled.

Kate nodded quickly. 'You said just now that the killer could be working with Copely, Guv – and where does Copely work? The library! That would explain why the tape was otherwise unmarked. It could have been purchased as part of a bulk supply of stationery and still sealed in its plastic bag when it was dumped in a drawer at the reception desk.

Copely himself may have actually been the first assistant to use it when the existing reel ran out and by doing so left his prints on the tape. The killer could then have borrowed it from him or snaffled the whole reel for his own purposes before anyone else got to handle it—'

Roscoe's snort cut her off. 'An even wilder bloody card,' he growled. 'We're getting into the realm of fairy stories now.'

Ansell nodded thoughtfully. 'Oh, I don't know,' he murmured. 'It's certainly a plausible scenario.'

There was a glint of excitement in Kate's eyes. 'You bet it is,' she exclaimed, forgetting herself for a moment, 'and there seems to be a definite link between these murders and the library itself.'

Despite his initial support, Ansell seemed taken aback by her sudden gush of enthusiasm and he made an irritable grimace. 'Then you'll know where your next line of inquiry will be, won't you, Sergeant?' he said drily. 'And when you *do* visit the library, perhaps you'll take Mr Fallow's book with you. One of the library assistants has just telephoned the incident room to demand it be returned forthwith – on pain of a hefty fine!'

The library was closed when Kate got there, following another non-productive incident room briefing, and she swore as she peered through the darkened windows at the rows of books in their tight aisles. Pink Glasses was nowhere to be seen and a check at the back of the building revealed that the car park was completely empty. Glancing at her watch, Kate saw that it was already after eight in the evening, so the fact that the staff had all gone home was hardly surprising. She hadn't realized it was so late.

Returning to her car, Kate sat there for several minutes, thinking about her next move. Plainly, the inquiries at the library would have to wait until the following day. Now, though, a quick trip to the chippy for a bag of their finest chunky cuts and a piece of battered cod – or whatever else it was they sold as cod – was on the agenda. Her stomach felt as though her throat had been cut and she needed something substantial inside her, like yesterday.

After that, there might be an opportunity to slope off to see how Hayden was getting on after learning of the murder of his favourite nurse, which must by now have become the talk of the hospital. She smiled grimly. That would hardly aid his recovery but he would find out soon enough from the newspapers delivered to the hospital anyway.

The local chippy was almost empty when she pushed through the glass door into the small tiled reception area and the smell of frying that greeted her stirred her stomach juices with rumbles of anticipation as she put in her order.

Minutes later she was back in the Mazda and heading out of town in the direction of the village of Watchfield, her monster bag of fish and chips on the passenger seat beside her filling the car with its unique aroma that she knew would take a couple of days to get rid of.

For a change, no mist floated in her headlights when she turned off the main Wedmore road on to the Levels and the moon was already thrusting itself up into the pencil-thin bar of fading light that for the moment still defined the horizon. A couple of black winged shapes almost grazed the car's windscreen as she entered Burtle village and something – possibly a fox – fled into the dusk at the far end of her drive as the wheels of her Mazda crunched into the gravel sideway.

Trudging along the path to the porch, she unlocked the front door and fumbled inside for the living-room light switch, relieved when the light sprang into life and the pale yellow glow seeping over the doorstep revealed that there were no parcels waiting for her this time. Maybe the killer was having a night off, she thought grimly, and, walking through to the kitchen, she dumped the packet of fish and chips on the work surface while she bent down to search for a plate in a low-level cupboard.

She heard the faint thud above her head as she propped herself on one of the bar stools at the breakfast bar and froze, a fork laden with battered fish halfway to her lips.

Carefully sliding off the bar stool, she kicked off her shoes and crept stocking-footed back into the living room, straining her ears for a repeat of the unfamiliar sound. It was an old cottage, always full of strange creaks and groans but for some reason the sound she had heard this time had grated on her senses.

She paused at the bottom of the staircase, head on one side and heart thumping. Then, quite suddenly, there it was again – like a heavy footfall – and, peering up into the gloom, she saw a trickle of light to the right of the landing. Someone was in her bedroom!

The risers made hardly any sound as she mounted the staircase, one stair at a time, and the fact that her intruder seemed totally unaware of her approach was indicated by more movements from inside the bedroom. Surely he had heard her arrive in her car and open the front door? Was he deaf?

She got to the bedroom door, which was half open, and peered into the room. The bedside light was on and a shadow was thrown across the opposite wall, a shadow which appeared to be that of a heavily built man, who was obviously moving about at the other end of the room, hidden from her by the half-open door.

She was about to push the door fully open when the voice called out, 'Leave any chips for me then?'

She released her pent-up breath in a loud gasp and straightened as Hayden hobbled into view from behind the door, a big grin on his good-natured face.

'How the hell did you get here?' she rapped. 'You scared me half to death.'

'Well, I didn't walk from the hospital,' he said, tapping the aluminium stick he was leaning on with the toe of one foot. 'No, a nice ambulance crew dropped me off about an hour ago.'

She studied his rumpled grey trousers and shapeless green cardigan and shook her head with undisguised disapproval. 'You should never have been discharged from hospital,' she snapped. 'It's bloody ridiculous.'

'I've got all the right tablets and a nice corset to wear, so what more could any red-blooded male want?' he joked, then frowned. 'Anyway, I couldn't stay there when the sister told me about poor little Claire Topping – and I was worried about you.'

'Me?' she snorted. 'I'm quite capable of looking after myself – and what use do you think you would be in your present state anyway?'

'I could always clock 'em wiv me stick, love,' he said in a terrible Cockney accent.

'You should be in bed, you fool,' she retorted.

He raised an eyebrow. 'Is that an invitation?'

She gave a faint smile. 'No,' she replied firmly, turning on her heel. 'That's the last thing you need with a bad back and a nice corset!'

'It's either me or the chips,' he warned. 'Your choice.'

Her grin broadened as she headed back downstairs. 'No contest,' she threw back over her shoulder. 'It has to be the chips.'

CHAPTER 17

P INK GLASSES TREATED Kate to a critical stare when she pushed through the glass doors of the library after leaving her Mazda car parked directly outside with its two offside wheels on the kerb edge. At ten in the morning, the place was practically empty, just an elderly man reading a newspaper at a table to one side of the door and a middle-aged woman thumbing through a book in the 'Flora and Fauna' section.

Kate gave a tight smile as she thumped Fallow's book down on to the desk in front of the assistant with deliberate force. 'Your book – returned, as promised,' she said.

Pink Glasses snorted. 'Not before time,' she snapped, a tic in her cheek twitching irritably. 'I rang your superiors about it.'

'So I gather,' Kate responded as sweetly as she could manage. 'Thank you *so much* for the reminder, Mrs er. . . ?'

'Rundle – and it's Miss!'

Oh, what a surprise, Kate mused with a spiteful smirk.

The assistant picked up the book and carefully examined it, as if it were a priceless mediaeval manuscript from the British Museum, flicking through the pages and peering along the spine before setting it down on a pile of others to her right and turning to her computer.

Kate waited patiently as she took her time tapping in some information. Finally, appearing to sense that Kate was still standing there, her gaze switched from the screen to the detective's face. 'Yes?' she snapped in a sharp 'what is it now?' tone.

'I have a few questions for you,' Kate replied, 'if you don't mind?'

'What sort of questions?'

'Well, for a start, how many people work here?'

'Whatever do you want to know that for?'

Kate sighed heavily. 'How many?'

The assistant made an irritable grimace. 'Three assistants at present, plus the senior librarian. Anything else you want to know?'

'How many are male?'

'What's this – a sex equality test?'

'No, it's a straightforward question that requires a straightforward answer, if you don't mind?'

The assistant flushed at the reproof. 'Er . . . two: the senior librarian and a Mr Copely.' She glanced at her watch. 'And Mr Copely should have been at work long before now. I don't know where he's got to.'

She obviously hadn't heard about his arrest, and his subsequent release on police bail meant he was probably still at home in bed, so Kate quickly changed the subject, concentrating instead on her Sellotape inquiry, which in the cold light of day now seemed a rather infinitesimal issue to pursue, despite her conviction that it could actually tie the library into the murders. 'I see you're a fully computerized operation here, Miss Rundle but presumably you keep some basic stationery on the premises – pens, paper, staples, pins – that sort of thing?'

The assistant raised both eyebrows in astonishment. 'What has that got to do with anything?'

Kate's tone hardened and she started to lose what little patience she possessed. 'If you find my questions so difficult to answer, Miss Rundle, I am quite happy to speak to the senior librarian instead?'

That implied threat certainly went home and Pink Glasses swallowed quickly. 'Of course we have stationery.'

'And do you use Sellotape?'

'Er . . . yes, we have a roll somewhere. It's used to put up notices on the windows about forthcoming new novels or exhibitions, that sort of thing.'

'Where is it now?'

'In my drawer here, I should imagine.'

'Could you check to see?'

The question was polite enough but there was no mistaking the authority in the tone and, though the assistant tutted irritably, she jerked open the drawer in front of her and peered inside. Kate waited while she rummaged around for a few seconds, frowning. Then the woman shrugged and looked back at her.

'It's gone,' she said and sighed. 'It really is annoying the way people borrow things and don't return them. It was a new roll too, still sealed in its plastic bag, the last time I saw it – the old used roll had already been taken.'

'When did you last see the new roll?'

'A few days ago – I can't remember exactly.'

'So who do you think might have borrowed it?'

'Could have been anyone. Several organizations use the library for meetings in the evenings – writers' and readers' clubs, a conservation group and the local historical society to begin with – and the stationery drawer is never locked—' She broke off. 'Now, I really have to insist on being told what all this is about.'

But Kate ignored her question yet again, homing in instead on what she had said about local organizations. 'The historical society has meetings in the library?' she queried sharply.

Pink Glasses nodded. 'In the evenings. We have a room upstairs. They pay an annual fee and it helps towards the upkeep of the building.'

Kate pursed her lips. 'I'd assumed they met in a village hall somewhere.'

'They used to but it got too expensive for them so they started using the library about a year ago.'

'How often do they meet?'

'Once a month. '

'When did they last meet?'

The assistant consulted a handwritten card taped to the desk in front of the computer keyboard. 'Let me see, they were here at the beginning of the month – I believe that unfortunate Moorcroft woman gave them a talk then – and they're due to meet here again Friday week.'

'Do they have their own key to the library?'

Pink Glasses snorted again. 'Of course not. One of the library assistants remains on duty on a rota basis each evening to supervise their visits. We are very particular about security at the library.'

'And can you tell me which member of staff supervised that last visit?'

Her face twitched again as she turned back to her computer and rattled the keys for a few moments. Then she shook her head sadly. 'It would have been that poor Schofield girl.'

For a moment Kate simply stared at her. 'Melanie Schofield?' she exclaimed. 'You're saying Melanie Schofield worked here?'

The assistant nodded. 'She was a trainee. Chirpy little thing. Dreadful thing that happened to her.'

'Why wasn't I told this before?'

Another shrug. 'You didn't ask – and I don't see how it is relevant to the poor girl's death anyway.'

Kate controlled her rising anger with difficulty. 'That is for us to decide, Miss Rundle, not you.' Then she added, 'Did anyone form any sort of relationship with Melanie?'

Another snort. 'And how would I know that? She was just a nice friendly girl and very good at her job. Everyone liked her. Mr Fallow was particularly fond of her. Said she was like a breath of spring.' She treated Kate to a frosty smile. 'Such a nice man, Mr Fallow.'

Kate frowned, thinking that after these startling new revelations, she would have to reserve her judgement about the inoffensive little historian.

Will Fallow was cringing in his study when Kate knocked on his front door shortly after a hasty burger lunch and his dour unsmiling wife had no hesitation in showing her through, treating her husband to a hard glance as she discreetly withdrew.

'So why didn't you tell me you knew Melanie Schofield?' Kate demanded without preamble.

The little man swung his swivel chair round to face her and raised both hands in a deprecating gesture. 'I'm so sorry, Sergeant,' he said, 'but I didn't think it was relevant.'

Kate nodded but not in agreement, thinking how many times she had heard that excuse. 'So you didn't think that knowing a victim in a murder inquiry was relevant?' she echoed.

Fallow made a face. 'I didn't want you to get the wrong idea,' he replied.

'And what idea was that?'

He sighed. 'I hardly knew the gal. She was just a very helpful young lady who sometimes sat at the desk in the library while we had our meetings upstairs. I was horrified when I heard about her murder but I was concerned that you might think there was a connection between her death and the society, which wouldn't have been very good at all.'

'Why would I think that?'

He hesitated. 'Well, you seemed very keen on finding out all about the society and its members when we first met and I gather you have already interviewed several of them – Mr Copely was particularly upset about your visit.'

Even more upset now he has been arrested, Kate thought grimly. 'So you decided to withhold the information?' she said.

'I didn't withhold anything – you didn't ask me if I knew her anyway.'

Kate snorted. 'Let's not split hairs, Mr Fallow. You were fully aware of the fact that we were making inquiries into Melanie's background, yet you chose not to reveal your connection with her through the library and the historical society?'

'There was no connection as such – she was just the person we liaised with on a couple of occasions.'

'Yet you apparently went so far as to tell Miss Rundle you thought she was like a breath of spring?'

He wrung his hands, the sweat standing out on his forehead. 'All right, all right, I should have told you but I didn't and I'm sorry – what else can I say?'

She resorted to one last bluff. 'You can start by telling me about the Sellotape.'

He looked blank. 'Sellotape? I don't understand.'

'I believe someone from the historical society borrowed a roll of it from the library during one of the meetings and that Melanie Schofield may have been the one who gave it to them.'

She studied his face narrowly but there were no giveaway signs in his expression. He simply shook his head slowly, as if considering the possibility. 'I don't know anything about any Sellotape.'

'Are you sure? Maybe that is why she was killed.'

His eyes widened. 'Why would anyone kill someone over a roll of Sellotape?'

'I can't tell you that but there is a definite link between the tape and the murders of all three women.'

Fallow's jaw dropped. 'All *three* women?' he echoed. 'You're saying there has been another one?'

'You mean you don't know? Don't you listen to local radio or read the newspapers?'

'Usually, yes but I've – I've been busy working on my new book in the last few days and I've sort of shut myself away. I had no idea there had been a third murder.'

Kate nodded soberly. 'And there are likely to be a lot more unless we catch this man soon. If you are hiding anything from us, you will have their deaths on your conscience.'

'But – but I don't know anything else.'

Kate stared at him intently. 'Are you sure? Was there any member of your society who showed particular interest in either Melanie Schofield or Tamsyn Moorcroft?'

Fallow stared about him wildly, as if seeking inspiration from the walls. 'No – no, there wasn't anyone. They're all history buffs, middle-aged men and women. Melanie was just – just the library assistant.'

Kate was not convinced. 'I believe you know a lot more than you are saying, Mr Fallow,' she accused, 'and I want you to think very carefully about that.'

She turned towards the door. 'You know my telephone number. I'll wait to hear from you.'

Then she was gone, leaving behind her a very worried little man who had every reason to fear that his comfortable ordered world of books and archives was on the verge of disintegrating. But if Kate felt at all guilty about the effect her hard-line tactics might have had on him, she was given no time to think about it or about Fallow's shock revelations, for her mobile chose to activate even as she was climbing into her car.

The caller was Roscoe. 'Get your arse back to the nick,' he rapped. 'Copely's back on the agenda!'

CHAPTER 18

JANICE YOUNG WAS sitting at the table in the interview room, clutching a cup of coffee in both hands, when Kate joined Roscoe there twenty minutes later. The thriller writer was plainly very nervous and there was no disguising the glint of triumph in the DI's eyes as Kate sat down in the chair beside him, frowning her puzzlement.

'Miss Young has something very important to tell us,' Roscoe said.

He raised an enquiring eyebrow in Young's direction and she nodded quickly, taking a brief sip of her coffee. 'Well, it's like this, Sergeant,' she began. 'I'm afraid I was not entirely honest with you when you saw me yesterday about the bird-watching evening.'

'Oh?'

Young glanced at Roscoe, then blurted. 'Yes, I – er – didn't stay all night in that hide, you see. I decided to call time on our little adventure just after Neville left.' She hesitated, then made a face. 'Maurice is not the easiest person to get along with, you understand, and, well, he thinks I chatter too much. He was most rude about it. Told me to "dry up", so I left him to it.'

'What time was this?'

'Oh, about half eleven – maybe a few minutes later. Not long after Neville had left anyway.'

Kate looked even more puzzled. 'But why say you stayed all night when you didn't? Surely you can't have wanted to give him an alibi if he was so rude to you?'

Young shook her head, spilling some of her coffee over her skirt. 'I didn't realize when you came to see me that that is what I'd be doing. I had no idea he was a suspect in these dreadful crimes – you never said.'

'But why the fib in the first place?'

Young made a face. 'Pride, I suppose. I didn't want the rest of our little birdie group to know that I had given up so early. I would have looked like a silly old maid who was afraid of the dark – not good for my reputation as a thriller writer, you see.'

'Which means,' Roscoe cut in, his excitement showing, 'our friend Copely now has no alibi at all.'

'Oh dear!' Young exclaimed. 'I do hope I'm not getting him into more trouble.'

Roscoe worked at his most benign smile. 'Course not, Miss Young,' he soothed. 'Now, if you'll give us that statement, the nice sergeant and myself will pop around to see Mr Copely and have a little word in his shell-like.'

As it turned out, Roscoe was denied that opportunity. When he and Kate hammered on Copely's front door an hour and a half later, they were met by a tearful Mrs Copely, who told them she and her husband had had a monumental row over his constant nocturnal absences. As a result, he had stormed out of the house and she had no idea if he would ever be back.

'I – I'm sure he's got another woman and he's with her,' she stammered. 'It's happened before, you know but he promised me it was the last time.'

'Any idea where he might have gone?' Roscoe queried.

Mrs Copely shook her head. 'Some tart out on the Levels, I expect,' she said with sudden venom. 'He likes them young and cheap.'

'Reckon he got wind of us coming, Guv?' Kate said as she followed her boss back to the CID car.

The DI nodded. 'Could be,' he replied grimly, 'but if the little turd *is* off on his toes, you can bet your arse I'll find him – wherever he's gone to ground.'

Detective Superintendent Ansell received the news of Janice Young's admission and Copely's subsequent disappearance with a characteristic lack of emotion, seemingly more interested in the information Kate had obtained from the library assistant than Roscoe's apparent 'score'.

'Still doesn't really add up, though, does it, Ted?' he drawled. 'I gather we're looking for a man with only three fingers on his left hand and, as I understand it, Maurice Copely has a full score of ten?'

Roscoe scowled. 'The pathologist could have made a mistake, Guv,' he said lamely, 'or Copely could still be an accessory.'

Ansell treated him to his most indulgent smile. 'You mean there could be two killers instead of just the one? Now that *would* be an interesting idea.'

His dark eyes switched their gaze from the DI to Kate. 'In any event, as you've suggested before, Sergeant, it appears that the library and the historical society are both key elements in this case,' he continued, 'and I think this Mr Fallow has a lot more questions to answer.'

Kate nodded. 'I will be seeing him again tomorrow, sir,' she said.

Ansell held up both hands, palms upwards in a deprecating gesture. 'Why wait?' he said. 'Why not bring him in now? Let's make our little author shit his breeches.'

In fact, Fallow did nothing of the sort. Like Copely, the writer was not at home when Kate called. 'Out researching some bloody site or other,' his wife snapped. 'Damned fool's obsessed with the past. Pity he wasn't more interested in the present.'

Then she simply closed the door and returned to whatever it was she had been watching on a television which was churning out some strident signature tune from somewhere at the back of the cottage.

Kate sighed. 'Tomorrow then,' she muttered to herself and went back down the path to where she had left her Mazda, intending to return to the police station to break the news to the charming Mr Ansell. She never actually got there, however. The bright yellow Volkswagen Beetle saw to that.

She had got as far as Mark village and was heading along Mark Causeway when the VW rattled past her, heading in the opposite direction. Ordinarily she would not have given the car a second glance but its bright yellow colour and the plume of smoke it was leaving in its wake, obscuring part of her road ahead, made it difficult to ignore. Then, as it passed her, she glimpsed the male driver, huddled over the wheel with his eyes glued to the windscreen, as if terrified that the road would suddenly come to an end right in front of the bonnet. Even without seeing the driver's face, Kate would have known who it was, for she had already recognized the car. She had seen it only a few days before, parked outside Will Fallow's cottage.

Slamming on her brakes and swinging round in an entranceway, she left a nice black mark in the road as she raced off in pursuit. She had no idea where Fallow had been – the library in Highbridge probably – and she had no idea whether he was heading for home and his 'darling' wife or somewhere a lot more exciting but what she did know was that he had an appointment with Detective Superintendent Ansell at Highbridge nick and she was determined that he was going to keep it!

Kate was intrigued. Fallow was obviously not going home, for he had turned off the main road at Mark Church and was cutting across the Levels in the opposite direction. She had originally intended trying to pull him over but the narrowness of the road made such a tactic far too dangerous, so she decided to reduce her speed to match his, hanging back and following him at a safe 'tailing' distance. After all, he would have to stop eventually, coupled with which she was now very keen to find out exactly where it was he was heading anyway.

That remained a mystery for several miles, however, and it would have stayed that way had not the brief flash of yellow through the hedgerows at the junction with the main Westhay road alerted her to the fact that he had turned right towards Westhay village itself. But if she had expected his journey to end in Westhay she was disappointed and a mile or so further on, well before the village, he swung sharp left into the mouth of a narrow drove, heading deeper into the marshland countryside towards Godney Moor.

Where the devil was Fallow going? This was really desolate countryside, with few habitations except for the occasional farm or isolated cottage, and if this was not a planned visit to some historical site, what else could the little man have in mind for the afternoon? Maybe he had been bitten by the bug and was out for a spot of bird-watching – or perhaps he was heading for a clandestine rendezvous with some hot-blooded local vamp? She winced at the unsavoury image her last thought conjured up and tried instead to concentrate on the road ahead, still keeping well back to avoid detection and following the trail left by the clouds of black exhaust smoke as they slowly shrank to the pot-holed surface.

It was a sensible tactic but one that had its drawbacks, as she found out when, just thirty to forty yards beyond a particularly dense cloud, it suddenly dawned on her that the VW was nowhere to be seen – Fallow had turned off somewhere. She had lost him.

Slamming to a stop for the second time, Kate jerked round in her seat and studied the flat semi-wooded countryside behind her. At first all she saw was a green-brown patchwork of fields, bordered by stunted trees and hedgerows and criss-crossed by streams. But then she glimpsed the puffs of smoke again, rising above a long low wall which struck off from the drove towards a collection of dilapidated-looking buildings about half a mile over to her left.

Reversing into a passing place partially blocked by a heap of loose chippings and wincing as her rear bumper tore into the gravel, she churned her way out on to the road again and headed back the way she had come, spotting the un-gated entrance to a driveway on her right almost immediately and pulling over to her nearside verge to take a closer look.

There was no sign of the yellow VW now, just a single puff of smoke hanging in the air close to the buildings. What on earth was a respectable local historian doing out here in this desolate spot? Visiting someone? The vamp maybe? Unlikely. Even from this distance, the buildings looked pretty lifeless.

She waited a few minutes to be on the safe side. She didn't want to be spotted before she'd had a chance of finding out what the little historian was up to. Then, turning into the driveway, she bumped slowly along the grassy surface, keeping her engine revs down and her eyes peeled for any sign of movement ahead. But there was none and she got to within a few yards of the cluster of buildings when she saw a gap in the stone wall on her left. It accessed an overgrown rear garden with a couple of derelict barns on the far side and, to her right, the ruins of what had once been a stone two-storey cottage with a tiled roof and tall brick chimney, which had seen much better days.

It was obvious that no one had lived here for a very long time and most people would have been more than a little nervous about visiting such an isolated spot, even in broad daylight. Yet timid little Will Fallow had driven right in without the slightest hesitation and it seemed more than likely that he had been here before. So what was he up to? It was hardly the sort of place for a lover's tryst, was it? There was only one way to find out.

Grabbing a small pocket torch from the car, she made her way round the side of the cottage via a narrow stony path to the front garden. The VW was parked a few yards away, just inside a gateway flanked by crumbling stone pillars but there was no sign of Fallow.

The empty windows of the cottage stared at her from scabby cracked brickwork sprouting a weave of parasitic climbers as she picked her way through weeds and low-level scrub to the open front door, and a strengthening breeze set a chain-like something clinking inside. She started involuntarily at the sound but then dismissed it when her gaze homed in on a small brass plaque attached to the wall beside the door. It looked to have been screwed into the stonework fairly recently and the inscription seemed to leap out at her.

'The home of Annie Laycock, 1788–1863,' it said. 'Burned at the stake for witchcraft.'

Underneath the plaque was a crude wooden sign, bearing the words: 'Danger. Keep Out. Site under restoration.'

For a few moments Kate just stared at the plaque, her heart racing and an uncomfortable chill creeping down her spine. Annie Laycock – Dark Annie? Suddenly she could see a logical reason for Will Fallow's visit; no doubt he was a key member of the restoration team. But the likely solution to the mystery about his visit gave her no comfort. The house had looked singularly unwelcoming, even from a distance and, knowing the sinister background of the old woman who had once lived here and the series of brutal copycat killings that had been committed since, she found the place about as inviting as an Egyptian mummy's tomb! Nevertheless, she couldn't just walk away from it now, not after following Fallow's smoking VW across half the countryside. She had to find him and satisfy her curiosity beyond all doubt. The most attractive proposition was to shout his name and get him to come out of the cottage to see her, avoiding the need to poke her nose into that creepy darkness but for some unaccountable reason a little voice in her head warned her against advertising her presence so early and instead she gritted her teeth and gripped the torch more firmly in one hand as she moved closer to the front door.

The door itself lacked a hinge at the bottom and had pulled away from the supporting frame, jamming itself in between two flagstones, and she leaned against it for a moment, head thrust forward into a musty smelling room to listen. Nothing at first, then something erupted from the gaping window above her head with a nightmare screech, practically giving her a heart attack, and showering her with debris from the sill.

Mouthing a curse over her shoulder at the magpie, which had now settled on a tree behind her, she forced herself through the door and directed her torch around the room, shielding the beam in her cupped hand to reduce its range and intensity. Two low doorways to her right and rickety-looking stairs, missing several treads, climbing up into a heavy gloom.

She moved forward cautiously, now less worried about the beam of her torch giving her away than walking into something nasty or falling through a hole in the floor. There was another open door at the end of the room and she took a deep breath and peered through – regretting it immediately.

It happened suddenly, taking her completely by surprise – a shape, darker than the gloom, slamming into her with all the force of a runaway bull, hurling her to one side as if she were nothing more than a shop mannequin. Before she could recover, her heel caught something on the floor behind her and she lost her balance and pitched backwards, her arms flailing the air helplessly. Hitting her head on the wall, she crashed to the floor with a bone-jarring impact at the same moment as the figure briefly blotted out the grey oblong of the front doorway before disappearing into the garden beyond.

In her groggy state, her head on fire from contact with the rough wall, she was only just conscious of the roar of the high-revving engine and the scraping, tearing sound of tyres biting deeply into soft earth as the powerful car sped away past the cottage from the opposite side. She managed to get on to her hands and knees and probe the gloom with outstretched fingers until she touched the wall again, then slowly palmed herself upright with the flat of both hands against the cold stonework. But by the time she made it to the front door, the car was gone, leaving just the rich oily burn from its exhaust hanging in the still air and the brief flash of sunlight on a windscreen between the hedges of the drove as it sped away towards the main Westhay road.

She saw the man with the bicycle a second later. He had shrunk back against the wall on one side of the drove, his bicycle in front of him, as if intending to use it as a shield and, despite the hammering pain in her head, she stumbled over to him.

'You OK?' she gasped, the fingers of one hand pressed against her temple, which was bleeding.

He nodded. 'Bloody madman!' he exclaimed, in a distinct Somerset accent. 'Nearly 'ad me, 'e did. Wha's 'appened to 'e then?'

She didn't answer him but clutched at the top of the wall for support. 'Did you get his number?'

He shook his head. 'Goin' too fast.'

'Any idea what sort of car it was?'

'Couldn't say, my duck. One of them low sporty things, tha's all I know. Bright red, it were.'

'What, a sports car, you mean? Soft or hard top?'

He scowled. 'An' 'ow would I know? Don't 'ave one meself. Been a 'drover or a tractor, could've said but not tha'.' He studied her suspiciously. 'An' what you doin' 'ere anyways?'

Kate produced her warrant card with a shaky hand. 'I might ask you the same question, Mr. . . ?'

'Rose,' he said. 'Albert Rose. My land, this, an' I were passin' when I sees Mr Fallow's car by the cottage an' went to ask if 'e needed anythin' – renovatin' old Annie's place, see, him an' tha' society—'

But Kate was no longer listening to him, as she remembered Will Fallow. Where the hell was the little man? He must have heard the car roar away, yet he hadn't materialized and his car was still parked in the same spot.

With a dreadful sense of foreboding, she stumbled back to the house, leaving the old farmer staring after her.

Her torch was lying where it had fallen, its beam focused on one wall. Groaning as pain rippled through her head when she bent over, Kate snatched it up, calling out wildly at the same time. 'Will? Will Fallow?'

But there was no reply and when she stepped gingerly through the door from which her assailant had burst just moments before, she could see why.

The room looked as though it had once been a kitchen of sorts and the big iron hooks from which hams and poultry had been hung in days gone by still projected downwards from the naked beams where the ceiling had once been. One of those hooks had been used for quite a different purpose now, however. In fact the hook itself was only just visible, exiting as it did through the back of Will Fallow's neck after passing through the underside of his jaw, leaving him hanging there like the raw dripping carcass of one of the animals that had once hung there itself.

CHAPTER 19

HAYDEN LEWIS'S FACE wore a worried frown as he studied Kate in the glow of the newly lit fire, holding both her hands in his own as a sign of reassurance. The cut to her head had long since stopped bleeding but her auburn hair was grotesquely matted around the wound and the ugly bruises down one side of her face were already clearly visible.

As with all her previous updates, he had listened in silence to everything she'd had to say about the day's events and, in particular, her encounter with Will Fallow's killer but now she had finished, his rebuke, if gentle, was none the less pointed. 'Another close call, eh, old girl?' he said. 'You really ought to be more careful, you know.'

She nodded grimly, freeing her hands and reaching for the glass of red wine he had poured for her. He was right, of course. She had only just escaped with her life during the Twister episode two years before and this last incident had been a bit like history repeating itself.

It was several hours since her horrific discovery at Annie Laycock's cottage and it was now pitch black outside, with a full moon rising. She had felt more than a little guilty about having to quit the crime scene while Ansell, Roscoe and the SOCO team continued to work on under powerful floodlights but Ansell had given her no choice, ordering her home when she'd refused to get herself checked out at the local hospital and telling her not to return to duty until she had fully recovered. To be fair, she knew that his decision had been the right one, whether she liked it or not – after her nasty bang on the head, she certainly needed a good night's rest if she was to be of any use to the team in the morning – but being sent home like a naughty schoolgirl really rankled and she had difficulty managing the resentment and frustration it invoked.

Sleep was the last thing on her mind too. Although dog-tired and still a little groggy, she knew it would not come easily. Talking things over with Hayden was the only way she could think of to settle her mind and get her thoughts into some kind of a logical frame – and Hayden certainly wanted to talk and to ask questions.

'So, what about this farmer who was nearly run over?' he said. 'Surely he must have seen more than just a red sports car flash past?'

She took a long pull on her glass of wine and shook her head, wincing at the pain that seared through her temple. 'Apparently not. Even when Roscoe re-interviewed him, he stuck to the same story – just a red sports car, was all he claimed to be able to remember. Couldn't even tell us the type of sports car or whether it was a man or a woman behind the wheel.' She smiled faintly. 'But even that was enough for the DI. He's really off on one where Maurice Copely is concerned – bit of a cause célèbre for him – and since Copely himself owns a red MGA, which seems to have vanished with him, Roscoe needs no further convincing that he is our man.'

'What do *you* think?'

She shrugged. 'Evidence we have so far seems pretty conclusive, I have to admit.'

'Except that he doesn't have a finger missing from his left hand, which could be a critical defence?'

'Roscoe reckons the pathologist could be wrong about that.'

Hayden gave a short laugh. 'Well, that's one way of getting over an evidential discrepancy – just ignore it and press on regardless. Any sightings of your man?'

'Not even a glimpse. He seems to have vanished into thin air. Wife says she has no idea where he's gone but is convinced it is with another woman, and he's made no contact with anyone at the library where he works. Could be anywhere.'

He sighed, refilled her half-empty glass of wine and poured himself another, blatantly ignoring the doctor's orders to avoid all alcohol while on the tablets he had been prescribed. 'So why stiff Will Fallow?'

'Your guess is as good as mine – and why in Dark Annie's cottage of all places? Bearing in mind what's been happening in the name of Strawfoot, that could be significant in some way. Trouble is I can't quite see how.'

Hayden sipped his wine slowly, staring at the flames in the open fire grate hissing and fizzing as a strengthening wind gusted rain down the open chimney. 'Maybe Fallow was implicated in the murders?' he said. 'Could be that he and his co-conspirator fell out?'

Kate shook her head firmly. 'No way,' she replied. 'Fallow's the last person I would see being mixed up in anything like this.'

'OK then, what if he was simply in the wrong place at the wrong time? You've said he lived for his local history and it seems the cottage where he died is currently undergoing restoration work. Maybe he happened to be out checking on the progress of the work when he ran into the killer on the site and was wasted for his trouble?'

'That doesn't explain what the killer was doing there, though, does it?'

'How about dossing? Your man may not be a member of the historical society at all but actually some psycho who is on the run and up until now has been sleeping rough at the cottage.'

Kate treated him to an old-fashioned look. 'A dosser with a sports car? Do me a favour, Hayden. I thought you were supposed to be a detective?'

He gave a rueful grin. 'Just a thought, that's all, and you don't seem to be coming up with any brilliant ideas anyway. Maybe Fallow's killing is not the work of your Strawfoot character at all but is totally unconnected with the murders of the three women?'

'I don't buy that either. With Fallow and Dark Annie's cottage involved, it is all too much of a coincidence.'

'So why go for such an elaborate method of despatch? There are easier ways of stiffing a struggling man than hoisting him bodily several feet up in the air to ram him on a meat hook attached to the ceiling – not to mention the strength that would be needed to do the job. '

Kate frowned. 'It's unlikely Fallow was struggling. According to the pathologist, he had a nasty impact injury to the side of his head in addition to the wound to the throat that killed him. She reckons he was struck with some blunt instrument before he was hung from the hook, so was very likely out cold when the killer finished him off.'

'Exactly my point. Why bother to stick him on a hook? Why not simply strangle him, like the women, or batter him to death? Far less effort required.'

'Maybe because the thing was personal. This was a particularly vicious killing by anyone's standards – unprecedented in its level of ferocity – which suggests to me that whoever was responsible was motivated by a sense of outrage. I think Fallow infuriated our man somehow, which is why he wasted him in such a sadistic way.'

'So you're saying this could have been a vengeance thing?'

'Or a response to blackmail. Perhaps Fallow put the squeeze on him and he took exception to it?'

Hayden nodded slowly, lips pursed in thought. 'That could be it but if it is, how did he manage to discover the ID of the killer?'

'I don't know but when I last saw him he seemed very uneasy, as if he knew something but was keeping it to himself and felt guilty about it.'

'That would put him pretty close to our man socially—'

'Exactly! Which brings us back to the historical society or the library – or both.'

'Usual suspects then?'

'But more than likely someone who owns a red sports car.'

'So Maurice Copely – but who else?'

'None of those we have seen up until now, so far as I know, unless one of them has a second car hidden away somewhere.'

Hayden raised an eyebrow. 'But your man Granger is a butcher so he's the most likely one to have cut his finger off at some stage, chopping up animal carcasses.'

Kate frowned again. 'I didn't notice whether he had lost any of his fingers when we interviewed him. That wasn't on the agenda then.'

He brightened, as if he had contributed something significant. 'Worth a check, though, wouldn't you say?'

She drained her glass and rose carefully to her feet. 'Probably but it will have to wait until tomorrow. I'm for bed now, I think.'

He grinned, draining his own glass and reaching for his walking stick as he climbed very slowly out of his chair. 'Excellent idea. Always ready for bed, you know.'

She studied him narrowly. 'To *sleep*, Hayden,' she warned him, reading the message in his blue eyes. 'Nothing else.'

'Course,' he said. 'Do you think I'd try and take advantage of a sick woman?'

'Yes,' she said bluntly, 'but since you even need help getting up the stairs and are strapped up like a bloody knight in armour, I don't think you'd present too much of a challenge.'

CHAPTER 20

THE TORCH AWOKE Kate – a shaft of white light tracing a path across the darkened ceiling.

Climbing out of bed, she padded to the window, her bare feet making hardly any sound on the thickly carpeted floor. The torch caught her in its beam as she pulled back the partially drawn curtains, but seemed to shrink, becoming a single headlight-like blaze in the shadows below before being abruptly extinguished. Then it snapped on again and almost immediately died – to blaze into life once more a second later. It was a signal. Her intruder was actually signalling to her! As she watched, the torch was switched on a third time and swung in an imperative down–up motion, plainly inviting her to join whoever was holding it in the garden.

Returning to the bed, she studied Hayden lying there on his back, snoring, with his mouth wide open. She was tempted to rouse him to tell him what was going on but decided against it. It would have been pointless. In his present condition, Hayden would be more of a hindrance than a help and, dosed up as he was on red wine and analgesic tablets to relieve his back pain, it was doubtful whether he could even negotiate the stairs. No, better to let him sleep.

Pulling on her robe, she made her way down to the living room. Her wellington boots were standing to one side of the front door and, slipping them on, she grabbed a heavy police-issue torch from the windowsill and unbolted the patio door. Then she hesitated, a familiar voice in her brain clamouring for attention, warning her to stay put. It could be anyone out there in the night and, police officer or not, she was still no match for a strong aggressive assailant – as she had found out at Annie Laycock's cottage. Common sense dictated that she should ring the nick and get a crew over to deal with things. Going out there on her own was plainly sheer madness.

She took a deep breath. Maybe it was but by the time a police team managed to get there, the intruder could be gone. Furthermore, it was likely that he would simply vanish at the first glimpse of a marked police car anyway and she knew she would never forgive herself for throwing away her one chance of finding out who was out there and why.

Her mind made up, she jerked open the patio door and stepped out into the moonlight, her torch levelled across the lawn at the boundary fence. There was no sign of anyone. She moved forward cautiously, off the patio on to the lawn, her torch following the line of low bushes marking the boundary on all three sides.

Then she saw the intruder's torch flash again from the far right-hand corner of the garden and, after a moment's hesitation, she crossed the lawn diagonally towards the spot.

He was just a dark shape, muffled in a hooded coat of some sort, and she now realized he was not in the garden at all but standing beyond it on the other side of the rhyne which bordered the rear of the property – well out of reach.

'Who the hell are you?' she began.

'Can't you guess?' Maurice Copely sneered.

Kate froze. 'Half the force is out looking for you,' she snapped. 'Running was a stupid thing to do.'

He gave a short unamused laugh. 'What did you expect me to do? Once that silly cow, Janice Young, decided to rubbish my alibi, I knew your lot would be around to pick me up. So it was either run or sit and wait to be fitted up by your boss, Ted Roscoe.'

'How did you know Janice Young was going to change her story?'

'A little bird told me.'

'What little bird?'

'Let's just say a friend. Janice apparently rang him, burdened with guilt over what she had decided to do, and he tipped me the wink straight afterwards.'

Kate thought quickly. 'That could only have been Will Fallow or Neville Haslar,' she said.

Another laugh. 'You suggesting I only have two friends?'

She pulled her robe more tightly about her as the cold seeped through the thin fabric. 'Only one, now Will Fallow has been murdered.'

'What?' Even in the moonlight she could see him jump. 'Will's dead?'

She snorted. 'Oh, *p-lease*. You know damned well he is – you were the one who stiffed him and you couldn't have chosen a more barbaric way to do it.'

'Me? Don't talk crap. Why would I kill Will?'

Kate chanced her arm. 'I've no idea but your car was seen racing away from the scene.'

He stared at her, his eyes white in the moonlight. '*My* car? That's impossible.'

'Not according to our witness.'

'Witness? What witness?'

'Local farmer you nearly ran down.'

He shook his head vehemently. 'I didn't do this. I haven't killed anyone. That's what I came to tell you. You must believe me.'

'How did you find out where I lived? Only the killer knew that.'

'I accidentally clocked you on the road this afternoon and followed you here.'

'Why?'

'I wanted to talk to you.'

'So why didn't you?'

'I thought it better to wait until after dark when it was safer.'

'But why me?'

'Because I thought I could trust you. I knew your history and how you stuck to your guns on the Twister case to make sure the right man was brought to book. And I suspect you're trying to do the same thing again this time.'

'OK, so talk to me now.'

'I already did. I've told you I'm innocent.'

Kate gave a hard laugh. 'And you expect me to believe that, just because you say so? The only chance you have of proving your innocence is to hand yourself in.'

He backed away from her slightly, even though the fence and the rhyne were between them. 'No way.'

'What, then?'

He hesitated. 'I think I know who Strawfoot really is.'

Kate's heart began to beat a lot faster. 'So give me a name.'

Another rapid shaking of the head. 'Waste of time. Your DI and his team are already convinced it's me. They won't want you to tell them anything different because they'll look stupid, so you're on a sticky wicket with your so-called colleagues – I need to get you some proof first.'

She emitted an irritable hiss. 'And how do you expect to do that?'

'By doing your job for you.'

'What do you mean?'

Instead of answering her, he came up with a question of his own. 'Do you read much?'

'Read?'

'Literature is the food of life,' he replied.

Kate stared at him, her bewilderment obvious. 'What the hell are you talking about, man?'

But a sudden incoherent shout put paid to any answer he might have given. It came from an open upstairs window of the cottage and, swinging round, Kate saw Hayden's tousled head thrust through it in the blaze of the bedroom light.

'Et tu, Brute?' Copely's voice said softly and when she turned back to where his hooded figure had been standing, she saw that he was gone, disappearing into the night as if he had never been there at all.

'Stupid!' Hayden rapped, his face pale as he leaned on his walking stick and stared at Kate in disbelief. 'To go out there on your own in the middle of the night? What were you thinking?'

Kate said nothing, simply stared down at her bare feet from the armchair in the living room and wriggled her toes. The two uniformed police officers, one the shift inspector, fidgeted uncomfortably in front of the open patio doors, nodding perfunctorily to another uniformed colleague as he emerged from the shadows of the garden with his torch, shaking his head. 'Long gone,' he declared unnecessarily.

Kate shrugged, thinking that it had taken the police units a good twenty minutes to get to the cottage following her phone call, so what did they expect? 'It's pretty easy to lose yourself out on the Levels,' she said. 'He's probably the other side of Glastonbury by now.'

The inspector nodded. 'We'll be getting along anyway,' he said, turning back towards the front door. 'Nothing more we can do here.'

Kate waited for Hayden's outburst as the uniformed officers left and it came even before they had actually managed to drive away.

'I asked you what you thought you were doing?' he blazed. 'I woke up to go to the loo, only to find that my wife was not in bed where she should have been but out in the blessed garden in just her nightdress having a conflab with a wanted killer!'

'I wasn't wearing just a nightdress,' she retorted sullenly. 'I had my robe on over the top. And we don't know if he is the killer.'

He raised his eyes to the beamed ceiling. 'Oh, for goodness' sake, don't split hairs, Kate. What you did was totally irresponsible. You could have ended up like one of those other women.'

For no apparent reason, she suddenly started to snigger.

He scowled. 'What the devil are you laughing at?' he demanded.

'You,' she chortled, 'standing there and giving me a bollocking in your little yellow boxers and T-shirt. Do you realize how stupid you look with your thin hairy legs and big belly?'

He glanced down at himself and grinned in spite of his anger. 'Don't change the subject,' he said. 'You were out of order and you know it.'

She sighed. 'And why was I out of order, Hayd?' she queried wearily. 'How was I to know who it was out there? I saw a torch, that's all – and anyway, if Copley had meant me any harm, he would hardly have advertised his presence the way he did. He came here to protest his innocence, that's all, and he took a hell of a risk doing it.'

'Don't tell me you believe him?'

She bit her lip. 'I don't know what to believe. There are so many ifs and buts in this case and Copely is too obvious a culprit.'

'From what you've said, there's enough evidence stacked against him.'

'That's just it – it's all too pat. It's as if we've been handed him on a plate.'

He leaned back slightly to park his behind on the edge of the sideboard. 'So who else have you got in mind?' he said.

She snorted. 'That's the problem – we don't *have* anyone. And there's something even more worrying, too. Just before Copely did his rapid foxtrot-oscar, he suggested that I couldn't trust my own colleagues – especially Roscoe – and that they wouldn't want their preconceived ideas about his guilt to be proven wrong.'

'He was probably just trying to drive a wedge in between you and the team – you know, bugger up the investigation by sowing the seeds of doubt in your mind about your own colleagues.'

'Possibly but he also said something really peculiar. He asked me if I did much reading—'

'Reading?'

'Yes, then he just said, "Et tu, Brute?" It didn't make sense.'

He frowned. 'It might have done if you had read classical literature at uni instead of those daft foreign languages.'

'What do you mean?'

'It's all about William Shakespeare. In his play, *Julius Caesar*, Brutus was depicted as Caesar's best friend and also the chap who conspired with other ne'er-do-wells to have him wasted at the senate.'

'So?'

'Well, as Caesar lay dying, after being fatally stabbed, he says to his treacherous friend, "Et tu, Brute?", which translates as the recrimination, "And you too, Brutus?" Maybe Copely was warning that you could end up being stabbed in the back by your own team to preserve the status quo in the investigation.'

'That's bloody ridiculous.'

'All part of the process of disinformation. Quite clever actually. Been used by politicians and military tacticians throughout history.'

He yawned. 'Anyway, I think that both Maurice Copely and Julius Caesar can wait until the morning. By the look of you, it's time you got some shut-eye.'

She also yawned and glanced at her watch. 'Point taken. Maybe we can get four or five hours in anyway.'

In fact they managed just three and a half. At precisely eight in the morning the telephone blasted through their dreams and, in her haste to grab the receiver, Kate sent her glass of water tumbling off the bedside cabinet on to the floor.

'What is it?' Hayden grumbled, hoisting himself up on his elbows with a long groan and staring at her bleary eyed.

Kate replaced the receiver with a shaking hand. 'Control room,' she said, her voice weak and strained. 'There's been another murder.'

'A what? Who?'

She met his gaze with a look of horror. 'Denise Haslar,' she replied. 'Neville Haslar's wife!'

CHAPTER 21

'I THOUGHT YOU WERE told to get some rest?' Roscoe growled when Kate joined him in front of the stable block after parking her Mazda in the allocated parking area with the half-dozen marked and plain police vehicles.

She nodded, even in the comforting gloom of the familiar marshland mist that had come with the dawn conscious of her poorly brushed hair and the dark smudges still lurking under her eyes, which she had seen in the bathroom mirror before leaving home. 'I tried,' she said tartly, 'but Hayden snores.'

He grunted, dropping the cigarette he had been smoking into the long wet grass and retrieving his chewing gum from the side of his mouth. 'Then maybe you should buy yourself some earplugs,' he suggested drily, adding, 'Have a nice chat with our killer, did you?'

Kate made a face. 'So you've heard?'

'Along with most of the nick. Must be something that attracts psychos to you. I seem to remember that that last nutter, Twister, had quite a crush on you.'

She bit back the response that flew to her lips. 'Copely came to protest his innocence,' she replied tightly. 'He said he'd had nothing to do with any of the killings.'

Roscoe nodded to the uniformed police officer standing by the door of the stable block and lifted a strip of yellow and black 'Crime Scene. Do Not Cross' tape to allow her to duck under it. Then he bent over to pull on a pair of protective booties he'd obviously stuffed in his pocket after coming outside for his smoke. 'Well, he would say that, wouldn't he?' he said.

She tugged a pair of similar booties out of her own pocket and leaned against one of the barn doors to slip them over her shoes. 'He took a hell of a risk coming to my place like that, though,' she pointed out. 'Could be he was telling the truth.'

Hauling open one of the double doors, the DI ushered her inside ahead of him. 'In your dreams,' he growled. 'More likely he shot over here to do another one straight after seeing you.'

There were four stalls to one side of the concrete passageway that ran from the door they had just used to another door at the far end of the block. Horses occupied three of the stalls but the end one appeared to be empty and two figures were bending down half in, half out of it – one suited and the other dressed in the familiar nylon overalls.

As Kate reached the open door of the stall, she saw that the body was of a woman in her forties, with shoulder-length blonde hair and the sort of slender, perfectly proportioned body most women could only dream of. She was naked, except for a blue denim shirt that had been pulled up under her chin to expose her breasts, and the bulging eyes seemed to be turned down and fixed on the grotesque straw doll protruding from between her bloodstained teeth.

'Ah, DS Lewis,' Detective Superintendent Ansell murmured, straightening up from the corpse. 'Recovered, I hope?'

She swallowed and nodded. 'More or less, thank you, sir,' she replied.

He gave her a zombie-like smile. 'Well, that's nice,' he said, the sneer in his tone suggesting he thought otherwise, and he pivoted round to wave a hand at the corpse, which Lydia Summers was still carefully examining. 'On the other hand, Mrs Haslar here is not quite so good, I'm afraid. A rather terminal condition, it seems.' He emitted a theatrical sigh. 'I don't suppose Maurice Copely mentioned that he might be coming over here after he'd had his cosy little chat with you, did he?'

Kate tensed but said nothing. His vicious sarcasm cut through her like a knife but she knew that Ansell was at his most dangerous when he was in this sort of mood and, despite the question he had asked, it was apparent that he was not expecting a reply.

His dark eyes bored into her. 'No, probably not,' he went on, answering it himself, 'but it was good of him to call by, wasn't it? Pity you didn't think to invite some of your colleagues to your little tête-à-tête, though, so we could *all* have a little chat. Then Mrs Haslar would have been able to look forward to riding again, Mr Haslar would not be in the state he is in at home and the unfortunate fourteen-year-old girl who came here this morning to saddle up her horse and found the body would not be under sedation.'

Kate still made no comment. She had to admit that, after Copely's vanishing trick the previous night, she was on a hiding to nothing – even though she bitterly resented her boss's attitude and what she saw as a totally unjustified attack on her professional conduct. What would you have done in the same circumstances, Mr Bloody Perfect? she thought. Stayed in bed with the sheets pulled up over your head and dialled 999?

She would have delighted in asking him that very question but, being honest with herself, she knew that she wasn't ready to look for another job just yet, and then the opportunity was gone when he abruptly turned his back on her, as if she no longer existed, and engaged the pathologist in conversation. His arrogant and very public dismissal on top of the sarcasm to which she had been subjected was calculated to humiliate and it certainly succeeded. Kate's hands clenched tightly by her sides and for a moment she simply stood there trying to control her involuntary trembling and hold back the tears. Roscoe scowled angrily. Tapping her on the arm, he caught her eye and nodded towards the door.

'That was out of order,' he said gruffly when they were outside, 'and I shall tell the boss that later, you can bet your life on it.'

'Thanks, Guv,' she said, taking a deep breath and staring across the field at the jumble of parked vehicles. 'But don't go out on a limb for me. Maybe I should just jack all this in now and choose another career. Ansell has made it very plain throughout this investigation that he doesn't think I'm up to it.'

The DI glared at her. 'Don't be bloody stupid,' he growled. 'He's under a lot of pressure at the moment and it's well known that he doesn't like women officers anyway. Best thing you can do is to make yourself scarce until he calms down. Get on with some more inquiries. Re-interview Josh Turner and see if he's holding anything back. See Copley's old lady again – and Fallow's too if she's up to questions. Maybe they'll say more to another woman than they would to a hairy-arsed DI like me.'

Kate gave a pale smile, in spite of her downbeat mood. 'Didn't know you had a hairy arse, Guv?' she said, dabbing her eyes with a handkerchief.

He glared at her. 'Beat it!' he growled. 'And thank your lucky stars you're not likely to find out!'

It had begun to drizzle through the mist as Kate made her way back to her car and, heading for Woolavington, she sniffed her disapproval at the rivulets forming, breaking and reforming under the scrape of her windscreen wipers – the weather in tune with her own downbeat mood.

She had always considered herself to be fairly thick-skinned but Ansell seemed to be able to get to her in a way no one else could. Perhaps it was due to the fact that he had been privy to her breakdown on the Twister inquiry two years before and that she was trying too hard to prove herself and demonstrate she was now fully recovered. On the other hand, maybe his rather effeminate leanings put him on the same feminine wavelength as her, which enabled him to sense where she was most vulnerable and use it to his advantage. Whatever the answer, she knew she wouldn't be able to take much more of it and the sooner the case was over and he went back to headquarters the better as far as she was concerned. 'Talk about team management,' she muttered as she drove into Woolavington. 'That arsehole couldn't manage a piss-up in a brewery!'

Lights flickered through the gloom in the windows of Copely's bungalow when she finally pulled up outside, despite the fact that it was only mid-morning, and, predictably, the red MGA was conspicuous by its absence from the driveway. Pulling her coat up over her head, she ran the few yards to the front door, praying that Marion Copely would be at home and that the lights were not just left on as a security measure.

She was in luck, however, and the dumpy dark-haired woman came to the door immediately, the expectant look on her tired face dying when she saw Kate.

'DS Lewis,' Kate began.

'I remember who you are,' Marion Copely replied. 'I was hoping it was Maurice.'

Kate made a face that registered her sympathy. 'Can I have a few words?' she asked.

Marion Copely nodded and stepped to one side. 'I haven't seen him,' she said as she led the way through to the living room and indicated a chair with a wave of her hand. 'I don't know where he is.'

Kate sat down on the edge of an armchair, waiting while the other settled on the edge of the settee opposite and smoothed her grey skirt with one trembling hand. 'You told my DI and myself when we last called that you thought he was with – err – someone else,' Kate said finally. 'Have you any idea who that could be?'

A short bitter laugh. 'Anything in a skirt,' Marion Copely replied, 'preferably about eighteen to twenty.'

'I assume he took his car when he left?'

Another bitter laugh. 'His pride and joy, you mean? He thinks more of that car than me.' She shrugged. 'Take a look around if you want but you won't find him here.'

There was an internal door off the kitchen giving access to the garage and it was completely empty, a small oil stain in the middle of the floor the only indication that a car had ever been parked inside. There was nothing else in the place worth looking at and certainly no sign of Maurice Copley.

The shed also contained little of interest, save wall-to-wall animal and bird photographs, just as Neville Haslar had said.

Marion Copley waited in the doorway, heedless of the fine rain, while Kate looked around. 'Did you know Maurice had hidden those corn dollies in here?' Kate asked.

A loud snort. 'He didn't do any such thing. They were planted by someone to get him into trouble – that's what he said and I believe him.'

'Why would someone do that?'

'How would I know?'

'One of his friends suggested he might have bought them for you as a present?'

'For me?' Now Marion Copely was angry. 'That's not possible. Maurice may be a two-timer but he would never do that to me. He knows how much I hate things like that.'

Kate frowned. 'Hate them? What do you mean?'

'They are the work of the devil and I am a God-fearing Christian woman. I wouldn't have such wicked idols anywhere near the place.'

The answer caught Kate completely by surprise and for a moment she was taken aback by the vehemence in the woman's tone. 'Right,' she said finally, 'maybe I was mistaken but one further question: is the shed locked when it's not being used?'

'Why would it be? Maurice only uses it for somewhere to display his photographs. All his equipment is kept in the house.'

'Then anyone could have got inside without you knowing?'

'That's what Maurice has been saying all along – those dolls were planted in here by someone. Garden gate is never locked either so anyone could have slipped around the back one night while we were asleep in bed.'

Kate thought about that for a moment but said nothing one way or the other.

'Well?' Marion Copely went on. 'Now do you see what must have happened? Maurice is totally innocent. Tell that to that nasty inspector of yours.'

Kate gave a tight smile. 'I will, Mrs Copely,' she promised, 'and I'm sure he'll be interested to hear it.'

The words of the distraught woman were still ringing in Kate's ears as she headed away from Woolavington, end route for Wedmore and Will Fallow's cottage at Cocklake, her face set in a heavy frown. You could be right, Marion, she mused as a multitude of thoughts crowded her mind. Maybe someone *did* plant those dolls there but on the other hand, the revelation that the shed was always left unlocked would not in itself get Maurice Copely off the hook. He could still have left them there himself, then used the absence of a padlock as a convenient get-out. Furthermore, in evidential terms, the odds could not have been more stacked against Copely and the only single thing in his favour was the pathologist's contention that the killer had a finger missing from one hand – but even then, as Roscoe had already said, that was only Doctor Summers' opinion and she could have made a mistake.

For her part, Kate didn't know what to believe but unbeknown to her at that moment, enlightenment was soon to be hers and in a way that she would never have expected or wanted.

There were no visible tears in Will Fallow's cottage. His wife, Rosie, had received the dreadful news of his death from DI

Roscoe the previous evening and, apart from a slight gulp and a narrowing of the eyes, she had exhibited little emotion. She was the same now, reluctantly admitting Kate and showing her through to the kitchen where she appeared to be making bread or scones; showing no signs of distress and apparently carrying on with her life as normal. A gaunt woman in her late forties, with her hair tied up in a bun, there was an air of hostility and resentment about her that met Kate like a cold draught.

'What are you here for?' she snapped, without offering Kate a seat at the big oak table. 'Police have already been to see me with the news about William.'

Kate nodded. 'I'm very sorry about your loss, Mrs Fallow,' she said. 'It must have come as a terrible shock.'

To her surprise, the woman gave her a thin, humourless smile. 'Not really,' she said. 'I always knew he'd break his neck one day in one of his old buildings or fall into a rhyne and drown.'

Kate was taken aback for a moment and just gaped at her. Talk about the grieving widow!

Rosie Fallow seemed to pick up on her sense of shock and sighed as she began working at the dough in her basin with strong deft fingers. 'You have to understand, Sergeant,' she said, 'that for something like twenty years William and I have been living here as husband and wife in name only. His all-absorbing interest in the past had long since killed any togetherness that might have been there once.' She looked up and for a brief moment Kate detected something akin to wistfulness in her eyes but then it was gone as her jaw tightened and she resumed her pummelling of the dough. 'We had no real feelings for each other, you see, except a degree of tolerance but went our separate ways. Then, two months ago, to add insult to injury, I discovered that William had begun having an affair. Some woman at the local library – a Miss Rendle or Randle, something like that. So if you were expecting to come here today and find a grieving widow, I have to disappoint you. I'm sorry William is dead, of course but the man I once knew died a long time ago.'

Kate's head was spinning. Miss Rundle? Will Fallow had been over the side with Pink Glasses? That was a real showstopper. And there was she thinking what a nice inoffensive little man he was.

'How did you find out about this affair?' she said, trying to conceal her excitement.

Rosie Fallow glanced at her quickly, then returned to her dough. 'I suspected something was going on,' she said. 'You know, a series of phone calls from some woman that were always claimed to be wrong numbers, several late nights out, which was not William's usual habit, and a trace of lipstick on one of his handkerchiefs.' She made a brief attempt at humour. 'Not his shade, you see.'

'But how did you know who the woman was and where she worked?'

'Ah!' she said, half turning towards her with her hands resting on the edge of the basin. 'I decided to turn detective and when William went out one afternoon after a phone call, I did a quick 1471 and got the number of the caller. When I rang the number, I discovered I was through to the new Levels Community Library, so I asked to speak to a fictitious woman whose name I dreamed up. The lady at the other end said there was no one of that name there and gave her own name when I asked for it.'

Kate smiled her admiration. 'Did you confront your husband with what you had found out?'

'Good heavens, no. To be honest, I wasn't that interested in hearing all the lies he was bound to come out with.'

'He could have been collecting a library book he had reserved?'

She smiled again. 'Hardly, and I recognized his trollop's voice from the "wrong number" phone calls I had received. She had quite a posh clipped tone. Very distinctive.'

Kate nodded slowly, thinking that that fitted Pink Glasses to a tee. 'A couple more questions, if you don't mind, Mrs Fallow. When did you last see your husband?'

'Yesterday afternoon, when he went out in his car. I never saw him again after that.'

'Did he receive any phone calls – like from this Miss Rundle – before he went?'

Rosie Fallow wiped her hands on a tea towel and crossed the room to a large Welsh dresser. Picking something up, she returned to the table and held out a piece of paper that appeared to have been torn from a notebook. 'He didn't receive any calls but he did make one – about an hour before he left. Fortunately, he wrote the number down and left the note in his study, where I found it when I went in to tidy up. Looks like a local number but I have no idea who it belongs to.'

Kate took the piece of paper from her as if it was a priceless fragment of papyrus. 'May I keep this?' she said.

Rosie Fallow shrugged and returned to her dough. 'Be my guest,' she said. 'Anything else you want?'

'I'd like to have a look around his study.'

'Go ahead but you won't find anything of interest. He wasn't a very interesting man.'

And Rosie Fallow turned out to be right. All Kate found were books, photographs of what were probably historical sites and bundles of notes, which appeared to be a part-completed manuscript he was writing, entitled *Sacred Sites of Antiquity*.

Taking her leave of the lonely embittered woman, she returned to her car outside, but before driving away she called up the incident room on her radio and got Tom Green, one of the civilian operators. 'Can you get on to Directory Enquiries and ask them for the subscriber of a local telephone number for me. Call me back soonest, will you?'

'Do my best, Kate,' Green replied, taking the number off her. But, as he ended the call, he turned to Roscoe, who was standing behind him with a question written into his craggy features.

'Kate Hamblin – I mean Lewis – sir,' he explained. 'Wants me to trace a telephone number for her.'

Roscoe frowned. 'Why?'

'Didn't say, sir.'

Roscoe nodded. 'You should have asked,' he growled. 'Keep me informed.' And he didn't look too happy as he walked away.

CHAPTER 22

KATE NEARLY PLOUGHED into a tractor when she pulled out on to the main Cheddar road and turned towards Wedmore. So much information was whirling round inside her head that for a moment her concentration was not where it should have been and in the thickening marshland mist the big unlit Fordson had been just a looming shadow. Fortunately, the farmer simply contented himself with a very prominent 'V' sign in her direction as he lurched round the nose of her car and carried on towards Wedmore, and she accepted the insult with a shaky grin, forced to follow him for an embarrassing couple of miles, until he turned off through an open gateway.

So, naughty old Will Fallow had been seeing to Pink Glasses for a bit of rumpy-pumpy, had he? But how was that relevant to his last-minute phone call to whoever it was before he met his grisly end at Dark Annie's cottage? And why had the revelation about Marion Copely's feelings towards straw dolls, vis-à-vis her Christian convictions, seemed so significant when it didn't really alter Copely's status as the prime suspect anyway? Somehow she knew that all of it was not only relevant and significant but also connected in some way. Furthermore, though at present everything was a jumble of loose strands, like the red sports car and Maurice Copely's unlocked shed, she sensed that there was something else lurking in the back of her mind – some fragment of information she had picked up along the way – which would tie it all together, if only she could tease it out.

As it transpired, however, there were no more disclosures or revelations to consider for the second part of the day. The Turners were not at home when she called, with neither car in the driveway, and when she dropped in at the Levels Community Library, she found a tall Asian man in a white turban behind the desk instead of Pink Glasses, who turned out to be the senior librarian.

'Jane Rundle had to go home early – I've had to fill in for her,' he said, his eyes widening when Kate flashed her warrant card. 'Apparently a close friend of hers has been found dead. She was very upset when she left here.'

I'm sure she was, Kate mused, especially if, as her reaction to the news seemed to confirm, she and little Will *were* an item.

The librarian was at first reluctant to give Rundle's home address but did so after Kate exerted some official pressure. Not that it did her any good. No one appeared to be at home in the neat semi-detached house she located in a side street off the main promenade in Burnham-on-Sea and not even the neighbours responded to her loud knocking.

'Now, where the hell have you gone, miss?' Kate muttered to herself as she went back into the street and studied the upper windows of the house. 'Are you hiding behind the curtains, perhaps?'

But Jane Rundle was doing no such thing. In fact, unbeknown to Kate at that precise moment, she was walking into the foyer of Highbridge police station, white-faced and tight-lipped.

'Can I help you, madam?' the officer on the desk asked with a smile.

Pink Glasses nodded. 'I want to speak to the officer in charge of the current murder investigation,' she said.

The officer made an apologetic grimace. 'Sorry, ma'am but that won't be possible unless you have a very good reason. He's an extremely busy man, you see.'

'Oh, I have a good reason all right,' she replied sharply. 'Tell him I know who his killer is but I won't reveal his name unless I am given immediate police protection!'

Kate felt as if she had reached a dead end as far as her inquiries were concerned. She had gone back to the Turners' house but they still had not returned and their place had that dead feel to it, which suggested they wouldn't be home any time soon. Anxious to cover all avenues, she re-visited the Schofields and Ed Shearing, and, after getting a hostile unproductive response from both Daniel Schofield and Melanie Schofield's unsavoury boyfriend, she drove all the way out to Bridgwater to call on Philip Granger – only to meet another brick wall when his wife told her that he was out at a 'Masonic do'.

Her earlier excitement now dulled and reluctant to return to Highbridge police station to face Detective Superintendent Ansell, she headed for the one place where she could be sure of a sympathetic ear.

Hayden had a mouthful of cheese sandwich when she let herself in the front door and there was football on the big 42-inch television screen in the living room.

'Ah, Kate,' he said, 'what a nice surprise.'

She stared at the television cynically. 'Liar,' she said.

He threw her a pained expression from his armchair, muting the sound of the television but keeping one eye on the screen. 'That's not very nice, old girl,' he complained. 'After all the work I've been doing on your behalf.'

She stopped in the middle of the room with a frown. 'Work?' she queried, glancing through the open kitchen door at the crowded draining board. 'Was that supposed to include washing your dirty dishes?'

He sighed heavily. 'Not that sort of work, my sweet,' he replied. 'I'm talking work work.' Then he broke off to cheer at the screen. 'They've done it!' he exclaimed. 'Goalless draw, which means they stay in the league.'

Kate shook her head wearily and, slipping off her coat and draping it over the back of a chair, continued into the kitchen. There was no point trying to hold a conversation with Hayden when he was either watching football or looking at classic car magazines and she was actually halfway through making a cheese sandwich for herself before he finally tore himself away from the screen and hobbled into the kitchen, leaning on his stick.

'Pickle?' he said, removing the lid of the jar standing on the chopping board and holding the jar up in front of her.

'Hayd,' she said solemnly, 'you are a slob!'

He grinned. 'And you, old girl, are a very lucky detective sergeant to have old Hayd looking after you.'

She pushed past him into the living room, her cheese sandwich on a plate in one hand and a glass of red wine in the other.

He followed her back into the room and, bending slightly, lifted a sheet of A4 paper from the coffee table and handed it to her as she sat down in an armchair.

'As you know,' he explained, sitting down also, 'I am a classic car enthusiast – in fact, I used to own a Morgan before I got into old Jags – and I was very curious when you told me about the red sports car thing.'

Kate paused in the act of chewing and glanced casually at the list of names and addresses on the piece of paper, her plate perched on her lap and her wine glass starting to tip over in her other hand. 'Hayden, what is this?' she exclaimed. 'There must be thirty names and addresses here—'

'Exactly.' He beamed. 'All local residents who live within a six-mile radius of Highbridge. You see, knowing the background to these murders, it occurred to me that our – *your* – man had to know the area pretty well to be able to select his victims and move around with apparent impunity. Apart from that one sighting by your only witness, Daphne Herbert, and your own brief glimpses of him, he has been able to commit his crimes and return home without being seen by a soul, so I hit on six miles as a feasible radius for him to live and operate within.'

Kate frowned. 'That still doesn't explain—'

'Coming to that,' he interjected. 'Then I thought about the red sports car you were trying to trace plus my main love in life – after you, of course – which is classic cars.'

'It may not be a classic car. It could just be a modern sports car, like mine.'

'True but it was worth a check anyway. So I got in touch with the secretary of my local car club and got him to go through his register for me and pull out any red sports cars – classic or otherwise – he could find among his members. It was a long shot but that's the list he faxed me five minutes ago.' He frowned. 'Right in the middle of a penalty too.'

For a few minutes Kate pored over the list of names which filled the sheet.

'Don't know whether it's any good to you,' he encouraged. 'Haven't had a chance to look at it myself.'

But Kate hardly heard him. Instead, she gaped at the paper in her hand as if mesmerized.

'I've been blind as well as deaf,' she gasped, dropping the wine glass on the floor and spilling its contents over the carpet, then staggering to her feet to send her plate flying off her lap after it. 'It was so obvious and I just didn't get it.'

Hayden stared back at her, obviously startled by her reaction. 'Steady on, old girl!' he exclaimed, his gaze dropping to the red wine seeping into the carpet. 'Didn't get what?'

She ran one hand through her hair, shaking her head in frustration and stumbling backwards towards the door. 'Think about it, Hayd,' she exclaimed. 'The legend of Strawfoot, the straw dolls, the psychopath connection, "Et tu, Brute?" – we've all been played for fools!'

He grabbed the chair arm and tried to haul himself to his feet with the aid of his stick as she grabbed her coat from the back of her own chair and threw open the front door. 'Kate!' he yelled. 'Where on earth are you going?'

But she didn't stop to explain and by the time he'd managed to hobble to the front door, she was already in her car with the engine roaring. 'Hayd, I've got to check something out,' she shouted at him through the open window. 'Trust me.'

'So let me ring the control room?' he shouted back. 'Don't do anything on your own.'

'Don't ring anyone, Hayd,' she responded, reversing at speed out into the road. 'With Ansell on my back, this is my best chance to score.'

Then she was gone with a coughing snarl of the powerful engine, her tail lights snuffed out in the gloom like twin candle flames.

Roscoe looked up quickly from the pile of documents he was studying and glared at the civilian incident room operator who had materialized in front of his desk. 'What?' he said brusquely.

Tom Green was accustomed to the DI's grumpy personality and took a deep breath. 'I got that telephone subscriber information DS Lewis wanted, sir,' he said. 'Took a lot longer than I had expected. Trouble is, I can't raise her now – she's got one of our all-singing, all-dancing TETRA radios with her but she's just not answering.'

'What do you mean not answering? Didn't you leave a message?'

The civvy swallowed nervously as if he was being adjudged personally responsible for the situation. 'Yes, sir but you – you asked me to keep you informed.'

Roscoe grunted again. 'So keep trying,' he said. 'She's probably in a bad reception area. You know what it's like down here.' Returning to the pile of documents in front of him, he added, 'Shut the door on your way out, will you?'

The mist closed around Kate like a shroud as she negotiated her way through the network of narrow lanes and she had to use all her self-control to keep her foot off the accelerator and avoid spinning from the wet tarmac into one of the treacherous rhynes. Fuzzy lights appeared periodically and faded with a swish of tyres and once a deer bounded across the road in front of her, forcing her to brake hard.

But then her destination emerged from the smoky rain-washed gloom and she slowed to a crawl, looking for the house she was seeking. It appeared suddenly but she made no effort to pull up in the driveway. Instead, she drove on a few yards until she found a layby and pulled off the road, close to a wall.

She switched off and sat there for a second, listening to the rattle of the rain on the hard-top. Then, throwing open her door, she stepped out on to the road and locked the car behind her, shivering as a penetrating drizzle greeted her through the mist.

A huge articulated lorry trundled past as she approached the driveway of the house and she watched its glistening coffin-like trailer vanish almost as it appeared. She sniffed. It would be weather like this, wouldn't it? Bloody mist and rain; it was a curse of the Levels. Still, at least she could make her approach to the house without being seen and no one was likely to be out in the garden now anyway.

She was conscious of the fact that she could be totally wrong about things and knew she couldn't afford to make any more stupid mistakes with Ansell seemingly already out for her scalp. But equally, she couldn't afford to ignore what appeared to be irrefutable evidence pointing to the identity of the killer. If she was right and could prove it, she would be the heroine of the day; if she turned out to be wrong and messed up, she would be looking for a new career!

There were no lights on in the house, despite the gloom, and, as she got closer to the front door, skirting a familiar parked car en route, she could see no sign of life inside either. Her feet crunched on gravel as she made her way cautiously down the side of the place, heading for the garage, and she froze for a second, wincing at the sound and expecting a door to open somewhere and a voice to challenge her. But the silence remained unbroken, save for the swish of vehicles on the wet road. The garage doors were firmly shut but, following the outer wall, she found a side door and tried the handle. Unlocked. Brilliant!

Turning the handle slowly and holding her breath in case it squeaked, she eased the door open. The handle made hardly any sound but the door stuck, then jerked open with an obtrusive scraping sound. She waited a second, tensing for the shout that meant discovery but incredibly, nothing happened.

She smelled oil as she stepped through the doorway and produced a torch from her pocket, snapping it on and training it on the long low car that was parked there under an all-encompassing tarpaulin. Her heart racing, she gritted her teeth and reached down to haul the tarpaulin off the front of the vehicle – then stared, with a sense of shock and exultation, at the sloping bonnet of a sleek red Austin Healey 3000 sports car. Bingo! She had scored.

She was so wrapped up in her crucial discovery that she didn't hear the scrape of the shoes on the concrete floor at the other end of the garage and her first indication that she was not alone came with the sudden devastating blaze of the garage light.

The tall muscular man was standing by the internal door to the house, staring at her, one hand in his trouser pocket and the other gripping the door frame almost casually. 'And what the hell do you think you are doing in here, Sergeant?' Neville Haslar said quietly. 'Researching classic cars?'

CHAPTER 23

'CRIMINAL OFFENCE, BREAKING and entering, isn't it?' Neville Haslar went on before Kate could say anything. 'Bit of a bad example for a detective sergeant to set, don't you think?'

His face looked drawn and white and his eyes had the intense haunted look of a man near the edge; small wonder after the terrible news he had received about his wife's death. Kate felt sick, doubts about the validity of her suspicions now beginning to crowd her mind. What if she was totally off beam? How would it look, not only to her superiors but to the general public as well, if this latest faux pas of hers ever got out? She could already see the headline in the local rag, following her suspension: 'Police Sergeant Breaks Into Home of Murder Victim.'

She swallowed several times, then cleared her throat, conscious of the fact that he hadn't taken his eyes off her. 'I – I called to speak to you about—' she began but broke off and came out with a lie instead. 'I thought I saw someone in the shadows by your garage and felt I should take a look.'

To her surprise, he raised both hands and gave her a slow clap. 'Very good, Sergeant,' he sneered. 'Now that *is* quick thinking – load of balls but quick thinking nevertheless.'

He pushed the internal door behind him wide open and waved a hand towards it. 'I think we should have a little talk before I ring your superiors, eh?'

Kate swallowed again, then nodded, feeling stupid and vulnerable. She had made a huge mistake and she was quite sure he was going to make her pay dearly for it. What if he *did* have a red sports car? So did lots of other people and he had never been given the chance to deny the fact anyway, so it wasn't as though he had been trying to hide anything. As for all the other strands her mind had put together for her, nothing seemed to stand up to scrutiny anymore; it was all conjecture – putting two and two together and making five! Her only chance was to try and persuade him not to pursue a complaint. She tightened her mouth as she stepped past him through the door. Crawl, if needs be, she thought, that's what she'd have to do, even if the very thought made her want to throw up. After all, what other option did she have?

'Do have a seat,' he said, showing her to an armchair in a quaint living room with an inglenook fireplace and a low-beamed ceiling, now lit by twin table lamps. 'Place is seventeenth century,' he said, noting her apparent curiosity. 'Left to my wife by her father. Do take your coat off. Er . . . drink?'

She slipped out of her short coat, hooking it over one of the wings of her chair and threw him a quick sideways glance as he opened a small cabinet and produced a whisky bottle and two tumblers. She shook her head. 'No, thanks, not while I'm on duty.'

He gave a humourless smile. 'Oh but I insist – and we might as well be comfortable while you do your best to try and persuade me not to ring your superintendent.'

He poured two large measures and placed one tumbler on the arm of her chair. '16-year-old malt,' he explained. 'So you should feel honoured.'

Kate cleared her throat again and took a sip of her whisky, more to please him than anything else but also to calm her nerves. 'I – I can only say how sorry I am for trespassing on your property at this dreadful time,' she blurted.

A cold laugh. 'Now that *is* a Freudian slip,' he said, waving his glass at her and leaning casually against the fireplace with his other hand thrust in his pocket. 'It suggests you are only sorry for breaking in because my wife has been murdered; otherwise, it would have been perfectly OK.'

She shook her head quickly. 'No, I didn't mean—'

But he silenced her with another wave of his glass. 'Forget it; I have already.'

She felt encouraged by his reply. 'Then I can only say how much I sympathize with your loss.'

He took a sip of his whisky and inclined his head in polite acknowledgement. 'Yes, it *has* come as a terrible shock, I must admit – even though Denise and I have never been very close.' He saw her look of puzzlement at the comment and sighed. 'Lived separate lives more or less for at least a couple of years. She had her horses and I—' He shrugged. 'I had the historical society and – what is it you called it? Ah yes, twitching – I had my twitching. Does all this surprise you?'

She shook her head. 'Relationships can be funny things, Mr Haslar.'

He nodded his approval. 'That they can and ours was certainly not the best but now she's gone, I just wish we had tried a little harder.'

He drained his glass and promptly refilled it, leaning against the wooden lintel of the fireplace again, with the glass held almost nonchalantly in his right hand, while his left returned to the pocket of his trousers, fiddling with what sounded like a bunch of keys. 'My type of sedative,' he explained. 'Now tell me, why were you so interested in checking my car?'

She made a face. 'I told you I thought I saw—'

He cut her off with an impatient cluck of his tongue. 'Let's not go back to that nonsense again, Sergeant. If you were checking for an intruder, why would you peel the tarpaulin back off the bonnet?' He gave a short laugh. 'I wouldn't think there was enough room for someone to hide under there, would you?'

'I was just curious.'

'Aha, curious, were you? Well, it's a 1960 restored Austin Healey 3000 – my pride and joy. Satisfied now?'

He was playing with her, Kate could see that but why? What was behind his persistent questioning? Surely he had enough to think about with his wife's death, without worrying about her interest in his car, unless. . . . And it was then, with a sickening jolt to the stomach, that she was provided with the answer.

Up until now he had been holding his glass of whisky in his right hand and gesticulating with it, while his left was hidden in the pocket of his trousers, but suddenly he changed hands as he turned to top up his glass yet again, and immediately the realization hit her with the sickening force of a blow to the stomach. Neville Haslar had already admitted that he and his wife had not been very close and ordinarily that could have explained why he was not wearing a wedding ring but there was almost certainly a more physical reason for the lack of the customary gold band – the finger on which he would normally have worn it was just a stump!

Kate took a more substantial gulp of her whisky, all but emptying the glass, every fibre of her being tingling with a mixture of fear and excitement. She was right about Haslar, had to be – it was too much of a coincidence – and the jigsaw pieces fitted together exactly, just as she'd expected them to when she had acted on her reckless impulse to check out his garage. His easy convivial manner had thrown her for a moment, giving rise to doubts in her own mind about her suspicions but she knew now that she had been right all along – Neville Haslar was Strawfoot and she was trapped in the living room of a murderous psychopath.

Almost too casually, she took another sip of her whisky and reached forward, ostensibly to place her nearly empty tumbler on the coffee table, which occupied the centre of the room, while her body tensed for the lunge for the door she knew she would have to make when the opportunity arose.

But then he was facing her again, his glass fully charged, and watching her with a faint smile playing about his thin lips, almost as if he could read her mind.

'Why, your hands are trembling, Sergeant,' he said, suddenly stepping forward and bending down to grip her wrist tightly for a moment. 'Surely I don't make you feel nervous, do I?'

Kate gently prised her wrist free and forced herself to sit back in the chair. 'Not at all, Mr Haslar,' she said. 'I'm just a little chilly, that's all.'

His sharp blue eyes fastened on her face for a moment before he straightened up and took her glass back to the cabinet. 'Perhaps a top-up is in order then,' he said, his back towards her as he poured her another whisky. 'They do say whisky has warming properties, don't they?'

But then he had wheeled round with a speed and agility Kate would never have thought he was capable of, blocking the doorway even as she sprang from her chair, whisky slopping from the glass he held in his hand and over the cuff of his shirt.

'You can't leave before you've finished your drink, Sergeant,' he said, his gaze dropping from her flushed face to her clenched fists. 'That would be oh so rude.' He nodded towards her chair. 'So why don't you just sit down again, eh?'

And there was menace in his tone this time as he backed away from her a few feet to kick the living-room door shut with his heel before setting the glass of whisky down on the coffee table.

'So my hunch was right?' she said quietly. 'You *are* the man we've been looking for?'

He gave a theatrical bow. 'Strawfoot at your service, ma'am.'

'So it was you who left those parcels on my doorstep?'

He shrugged. 'Well obviously. I thought it would make things a bit more interesting.'

'So why choose me?'

'Well, I didn't at the start. Originally the plan was to quietly deposit each parcel at Highbridge nick, addressed to the senior investigating officer but then in the afternoon after Melanie Schofield's body was discovered, curiosity drew me back to the scene of my crime – a lot of murderers re-visit the scene like that, I believe. Anyway, I saw you turn up and was immediately attracted to you. There were a lot of press reporters there and, professing to be a member of "the clan", I was able to learn from one of them who you were and that you were something of a celebrity after the Twister case. How could I not choose you after that?'

'But how did you find out where I lived?'

'Oh that was easy. The reporter also disclosed that you lived in a nice thatched cottage in Burtle with an eccentric colleague named Hayden who owned a red Mk II Jag. You had it made, he said – bit of jealousy there I think – but finding you as a result of his pique was then made simple.'

'As simple as setting up Copely to take the fall for you, I suppose?' she said bitterly. ' "Et tu, Brute?" – he couldn't have been more apt with his Julius Caesar quote, could he? Stabbed in the back by someone he trusted.'

He raised his eyebrows. 'Is that what he said? I never realized he knew Shakespeare. But, yes, you're quite correct. I have been quite the Judas – or Brutus, if you prefer.

'When I came up with my little plan soon after joining the historical society and reading about Strawfoot in Will Fallow's book, I happened to be running Maurice home, following an evening out at our local pub – my turn to drive, you see – when we were stopped by police on a routine check. Maurice was really hostile towards them and when I queried this later, he confided in me that he had a thing about the police after having once been wrongly accused by them of touching up little girls. He said he'd subsequently been acquitted but as mud tends to stick in such cases, I knew he would make the ideal patsy for me and it was surprisingly easy to set him up.'

Kate nodded. 'Like planting the straw dolls in his shed, fabricating his fingerprints on the parcel and making him look even more guilty by persuading him to run after you had convinced Janice Young to withdraw her alibi?' She grimaced. 'Ironic that the so-called friend who could have backed up his claim that he was in the hide bird-watching the night Claire Topping was killed had actually left early to commit the murder.'

Haslar chuckled. 'Oh, that flu thing was a stroke of genius on my part, I agree. It enabled me to slide away without any questions being asked – in the same way as it provided me with a cast-iron alibi for the murders of the witch woman and Melanie Schofield.'

'Strange how your wife never wondered what her so sick husband was doing wandering about the Levels in the middle of the night?'

He shrugged. 'Denise wouldn't have heard the sound of the roof collapsing,' he replied. 'She took sleeping tablets, you see, and was out for the count as soon as her head hit the pillow – coupled with which, we had separate rooms – so I had the perfect alibi. As far as she was concerned, her poor hubby was in bed all night. As for the daytime, she worked in Bridgwater from ten most mornings until about 5.30, so she would have had no idea what I was up to. A perfect situation for me.'

'Fabricating Copely's fingerprints on the second parcel you left me must have been more difficult, though,' Kate persisted.

'Oh, I didn't fabricate them,' he replied. 'He unwittingly provided them for me. You see, I actually visited the library – ostensibly on a research mission – the week before I contracted the bout of pretend flu that was so necessary to enable me to miss the witch woman's talk and I simply asked him for the loan of the library's Sellotape. Then I enlisted his help in repairing the tear in a document file I was holding – which I subsequently removed when I got home so I could re-apply it to my parcel later on. As the file was plastic, it was quite an easy thing to do too—'

'And you made sure he used a new unwrapped reel of tape so that no one else's fingerprints would be on it?' she finished for him.

'Oh, you *are* on the ball,' he murmured. 'But yes, I had earlier filched the library's own part-used tape from the desk drawer while Maurice's back was turned and substituted the reel I had brought with me, which was still sealed in its plastic bag. Then, after using the tape for my file, I conveniently forgot to return it before leaving, just in case it was a different brand to the sort normally supplied.'

'Why use it on the second parcel and not the first?'

'Had to, my dear, otherwise poor old Maurice might have been locked up before I'd completed my work – and I had to make sure he absconded once his alibi was withdrawn, not only, as you have already observed, so he would make himself look even more guilty but also to ensure he was still on the loose when my dear wife met her maker. Clever, eh?'

'Surprised an intelligent man like Maurice Copely didn't smell a rat,' Kate retorted pointedly, with the emphasis on the word 'rat'. 'Especially over the business with your file and the Sellotape.'

He ignored the insult, merely smirking at her again. 'Why would he?' he said and held up his left hand to show his missing finger. 'He could see that my disability made such a fiddly job difficult for me.'

'You mean you *made* it look difficult,' she countered. 'Your *disability* didn't stop you strangling four innocent women, including your wife, did it – *and* stringing up poor Will Fallow?'

His face noticeably darkened. 'Fallow deserved all he got,' he grated. 'The little bastard had been rooting around like a little ferret after the witch woman was found dead and somehow he must have worked out that I was the culprit – possibly because of the keen interest I had shown in the Strawfoot legend at the start. Instead of informing the police, however, he decided to try to blackmail me. Big mistake. I couldn't let that go unpunished.'

'Will Fallow resorted to blackmail?' she breathed.

'Oh, the money wasn't for him, you understand,' he mocked. 'It was to rescue his beloved Levels restoration project, which was almost boracic, and to save him and the historical society from public humiliation. Anyway, I arranged to meet him at Annie Laycock's cottage – which, I feel sure you'll agree, couldn't have been a more appropriate place for his demise. '

Kate shook her head. 'You're saying he was prepared to keep quiet about three murders in exchange for cash? I don't believe you.'

'Believe what you like, Sergeant,' he replied, 'but I have no reason to lie to someone who will also be dead very shortly!'

Haslar was only putting into words what Kate knew already but she should still have suffered a sense of shock at his chilling matter-of-fact statement. Instead, she simply stared at him, as if having difficulty taking in what he had just said. For some reason, she was getting very warm and finding it difficult to focus on his face. Damned whisky, she thought, and shook her head several times to try and clear the woolly feeling that seemed to be trying to clog her brain.

'But why – why were those women killed in the first place?' she said, her voice now sounding thick and distant as the room seemed to expand and contract around her.

'Ah but they were all part of the grand plan,' he said. 'Resurrect a local legend and convince the police that they are dealing with a psychopath who is hooked on the story of Martha Tinney and obsessed with the desire to carry out a series of copycat killings. Then, when the wife of a respectable local businessman is murdered in the same way as the other women, it would be accepted that she is just another victim of the deranged killer.' Another smirk. 'Got right into the part too. Even dressed up in all the appropriate gear to give it a bit of authenticity, just in case I was spotted by someone, In fact, I made sure I *was* seen by one passing motorist when I did Melanie Schofield, just to reinforce my message, which I gambled on you and your colleagues picking up sooner or later when the witness came forward.'

Kate swayed slightly in her chair. 'But your wife?' she said, conscious of the fact that she was finding it difficult to phrase words. Shit! She felt drunk – wrong time and place for that! 'You – you killed all those innocent women just so you could murder your wife?'

He shrugged. ''Fraid so, Sergeant. The witch woman had to go first, of course. I'd already learned from Fallow that she was one of the few people who still actually made the straw dolls I needed and it made sense to waste her at the same time as I was helping myself.'

'And – and Melanie Sch-Schofield?'

'Ah, she was a gift. The historical society usually held its meetings at the library where she worked as an assistant, you see, so I'd got to know her pretty well – I think she saw me as a kind of agony aunt whom she could confide in. Anyway, shortly after I had gone down with my pretend flu then topped the witch woman, little Melanie actually rang me at home to see if my flu was any better.' His smirk broadened. 'So very touching – and also very helpful to me in selecting my next victim, for she happened to mention in conversation that she was going to a friend's birthday party the following night in my village. She said she was a bit worried about going home afterwards because her parents would be out and her boyfriend was apparently a heavy drinker, which meant she was likely to be walking back. I knew this was one opportunity I just couldn't pass up.'

'You – you scumbag!' Kate mumbled.

He ignored the insult. 'A lot of waiting around, of course but it all worked out for the best in the end – and I was lucky too. I had no idea until I picked up some village gossip afterwards that she had a boyfriend who would ordinarily have run her home had they not fallen out.'

Kate squeezed her eyes shut and shook her head to try and clear away the fug that was developing. 'And Claire Topping?' she jerked out with even more difficulty.

'Oh, I'm afraid her selection was down to you, my dear. You see, the evening you ran Nursey home, I had popped by your little cottage to quietly drop off that first parcel but saw you actually driving away as I arrived. Out of curiosity, I decided to see what you were up to and, after quickly dumping the parcel on your doorstep, I followed you all the way to the hospital, then back to Mark again afterwards. When you dropped that pretty little thing off, it was as if you had picked my next target for me. Sort of providential.'

Having already suspected that that was the case, the cruel revelation cut right into Kate, despite her increasingly muddled senses but somehow she knew she had to bury her feeling of guilt for the time being and concentrate on getting answers from him while she could – even if, in the final analysis, she never got the chance to do anything with the information.

'But – but your own wife. What. . . ?'

Her voice trailed off as the room swam and he strolled over to her and bent down in front of the chair to stare intently into her face. 'Money, my dear,' he said softly. 'The root of all evil, as they say.' He drained his glass without taking his eyes off her. 'My business was in serious financial difficulties, you see – facing bankruptcy in a couple of months, which I just couldn't allow. So, in preparation for my Strawfoot debut, I took out a hefty insurance policy on the lovely Denise.' He straightened up and collected Kate's whisky glass from the coffee table, adding, 'And the pay-out on that will solve all my problems once the inquest and Copely's conviction are out of the way. All nice and tidy.'

Kate tried to hoist herself up in her seat but somehow couldn't make her legs work properly. Her senses were really spinning now and his face seemed to have become horribly distorted, his voice booming at her as he thrust a small pill bottle under her nose. 'Sedatives prescribed by the nice doctor to ease my trauma,' he said. 'I'm afraid I rather overdosed your whisky.'

Kate forced her eyes to focus and gripped the chair arms tightly. 'Killing police officer . . . they'll throw – throw away the key,' she heard herself gasp breathlessly.

He laughed again. 'Who will know, my dear?' he said. 'They'll never find you at the bottom of a peat bog and the Levels have an absolute abundance of those.' He frowned suddenly. 'Need to get hold of your car first, though. Have to get rid of it somewhere afterwards.'

He bent over her chair and she was vaguely aware of him rummaging through the pockets of her coat, then producing her keys and straightening up with a grunt of satisfaction. 'Leave the old MX5 in the road, did you?' his voice boomed.

'Killing me won't – won't do you any good,' she whispered as, despite her fading senses, she remembered the tell-tale deformity to his left hand. 'You've . . . already . . . shit out.'

His face was right up close to hers now, and she saw uncertainty and a hint of panic in his blue eyes. 'Shit out? What do you mean?'

She gave a humourless chuckle. 'You've . . . fingered . . . fingered yourself . . . arsehole,' she said in a hesitant slurred voice and before he could question her further, the black pit, which had opened up before her, swallowed her whole.

CHAPTER 24

JANE RUNDLE WAS sitting on the edge of her chair in the interview room when Roscoe walked in. She was plainly very nervous and he could see that the thin veined hands gripping the cup of coffee on the table in front of her were trembling slightly.

She looked up when she heard the door open, studying him owlishly through her large pink glasses, and frowned when he introduced himself in his usual brusque fashion. 'I wanted the officer in charge,' she said. 'Is that you?'

Roscoe was tired and he scowled at her. 'The boss is at headquarters,' he retorted. 'It's me or nothing, love. Now, what's this about knowing the ID of the man we are looking for?'

She grunted, gulped some coffee, then stared into her mug. 'I want your assurance that I will receive police protection before I say a word.'

Roscoe dumped himself in the other chair. 'Listen, Mrs Rundle—'

'Miss!'

'*Miss* Rundle, we don't have the resources to provide police protection unless there is a very specific reason for it. Your best protection is telling us what you know, so we can arrest this man and put him away where he belongs.'

She thought for a second. 'There's something else too – I want immunity from prosecution.'

Roscoe looked confused. '*You* want immunity? Immunity for what?'

'Blackmail,' she said simply and waited until he closed his mouth before continuing. 'Mr Fallow, God rest his soul, had suspected this man as being the culprit for some time. I don't know how he found out but he told me who it was and that he intended making him pay – literally. He was going to set up a meeting—'

'Annie Laycock's cottage?'

She nodded. 'And tell him unless he paid a substantial sum, Will would go to the police.'

'You were prepared to let a multiple murderer off the hook for *money*?'

'It wasn't like that. You have to understand that Will was devoted to his restoration project for the Levels' ancient sites and he desperately needed the money to prevent the whole thing failing. Once he had got his money, he fully intended tipping the police off about the man by an anonymous phone call.'

'And that made it all right, did it?'

'Of course not but Will was dead set on the idea. I tried to change his mind but he wouldn't hear of it.'

'And why did Fallow confide in you in the first place?'

She fidgeted uncomfortably. 'We – we had a thing going between us.'

'A married man? All a bit sordid, isn't it?'

'I know it was wrong but—'

Roscoe sighed heavily. 'I'm not interested in your moral behaviour, Miss Rundle, and I don't think CPS will do anything about the blackmail issue – Fallow's dead now anyway.' He leaned forward, staring at her intently. 'What I do need, however, is the name of this psychopath before he kills again.'

She bit her lip, hesitating.

'The name, Miss Rundle,' he snapped.

'Neville Haslar,' she said. 'He's your man.'

Detective Superintendent Ansell stared out of the window of the SIO's office, thinking. Having been subjected to an angry 'get your finger out' tirade from the assistant chief constable in another short briefing at headquarters, he was not in the best of moods, and the pile of newspapers he had brought up with him from the station duty office – screaming such headlines as 'Bloodbath On The Somerset Levels' and 'Cops Without A Clue' – had only exacerbated his foul mood. Roscoe's briefing on Jane Rundle should have given him the shot in the arm he so desperately needed but Ansell was a careful, analytical man. The information looked good – too good, in fact – but it needed consideration. To jump now as a kneejerk reaction to the roasting he had received from his boss was unwise and definitely not his style. The last thing he wanted to do was to compound his alleged 'felony' of dragging his feet by taking ill-thought-out precipitate action that would end in tears.

'Want me to pick Haslar up, Guv?' Roscoe said, losing what little patience he possessed after several minutes' silence.

Ansell turned on him. 'What for?' he queried.

Roscoe looked bewildered. 'Well, multiple murder would sound about right.'

'And where's your evidence?'

'We've just got that from Jane Rundle.'

'No, Detective Inspector,' Ansell said sharply, 'you haven't got anything of the sort – you have an allegation from a distraught woman who was having an affair with one of the victims. You have absolutely nothing else – no forensic evidence, no witness ID, not even a positive link to any of the victims, except Fallow – and, if I'm not mistaken, Mr Haslar has a pretty good alibi for at least the first killing by being in bed with the flu! Rundle could be off her head or simply making the whole thing up to get back at Haslar for some reason.'

'But surely, Guv. . . ?'

'Surely, balls! Of course we should interview Haslar again but arresting him now would get us nowhere. All he would have to do is deny the allegation and we would have to chuck him out again but by then he would be forewarned about our suspicions and take even greater care to cover his tracks.'

Roscoe released his breath with a sound like a high-velocity round leaving the muzzle of an automatic pistol. 'So what do I tell Jane Rundle?' he retorted.

Ansell gave him one of his watery smiles. 'Just say *thank you* for your information, Miss Rundle,' he patronized. 'It will receive our urgent attention. OK?'

As far as Roscoe was concerned, it wasn't OK, for he had had just about enough of Ansell's demeaning remarks and was close to boiling point. But he was saved from what could have been a very career-limiting reaction by a peremptory knock on the office door.

'Sorry, Mr Roscoe,' Tom Green gulped, a familiar-looking computer print-out in one hand, 'but I am still getting no response from DS Lewis—'

Ansell wheeled to face the civilian operator. 'Kate Lewis? What do you mean?'

Roscoe glared at Green as if he had just contravened the Official Secrets Act. 'I gather she wanted a telephone subscriber traced, Guv,' he muttered. 'Some routine inquiry she was following up.'

'How long have we been trying to reach her?'

Green looked really unhappy now, like a man caught between two fires. 'It's well over an hour now, sir, which I felt was most unlike her, so I telephoned her home address and got her husband.'

'And?' Ansell snapped.

Green hesitated. 'It – it seems Kate – DS Lewis – left the house in a bit of a rush to follow up some lead on the inquiry and Hayden has only just discovered that she left her radio behind.'

Ansell hissed his disapproval. 'Do we know why she wanted the name of this subscriber or where she was going?'

Green shook his head. 'No, sir but Hayden said he'd given her a members list of red sports car owners from a local car club, and she apparently went ape when she took a look at it. I don't know whether that's connected.'

Ansell's face hardened. '*He* gave her a list? How the hell did he manage to do that if he was on the sick?'

The embarrassed civvy said nothing, so Ansell continued in the same angry vein. 'And why didn't DC Lewis report this before? Hells bells, he's supposed to be her bloody husband!'

Green hesitated, then said, 'He said she told him not to – something about needing to score.'

'Shit!' Roscoe breathed, now looking very alarmed. 'That means she was on to something important and didn't want to share the info until she was sure. She could be in loads of trouble.'

'This is what happens when officers do a Lone Ranger job,' Ansell snarled, snatching the print-out from Green and scanning the contents.

Roscoe scowled. 'Can you blame her, Guv?' he said. 'So far, every idea she's put forward has been laughed out of court.'

But the barbed remark was lost on Ansell as the name on the print-out jumped straight out at him. 'Get some units out to this address pronto,' he rasped at Green and, even as the civvy left the office almost at a run, he snatched his coat from the back of a chair and literally pushed Roscoe out of the office ahead of him. 'I hope you're up to high-speed driving, Ted,' he snapped, 'because Kate Lewis's life may depend on it.'

'So who was the mystery subscriber on that print-out?' Roscoe threw back over his shoulder as they left the incident room.

Ansell practically spat the name and pushed past him in the corridor. 'Neville Haslar!'

The DI threw him a sideways glance. 'Enough grounds for a pull now then, is there, Guv?' he queried grimly.

'Shut it, Ted!' his boss replied. 'Just concentrate on staying on the road!'

Pain, noise and blinding light. Kate groaned and tried to turn away from it all but it was useless. Someone was persistently slapping her face and yelling at her. Then her mouth was forced open and what felt like someone's fingers were forced down her throat. She gagged on the obstruction, then choked as her stomach reacted violently and voided its contents up out of her mouth in a burning torrent.

'Wake up!' a voice boomed. She could smell the acrid stench of vomit and now someone was shaking her violently by the shoulders. More stinging slaps to her face. She partially surfaced from her shadow world, then started to drift back. It was safer, more comfortable there. She didn't want to leave.

A white blob in front of her – a face? Then the blackness blotting it out. Someone swearing and hoisting her up. Was she lying down or sitting? She couldn't tell. 'We've no time,' a voice was telling her. 'Wake up, you silly cow!'

She felt pressure on her legs as if she were standing up but they were like plasticine and folded almost immediately. More hoisting, rough hands on her hips, visual images flashing before her eyes that lacked any real definition – walls spinning round and round, chairs and a table dancing like live things. Then she was conscious of being draped over something with her head facing downwards – something that moved fast and shook her up and down as it went. Was she being carried? On someone's shoulder? Where were they going? She just wanted to sleep. . . .

More visual images and she tried to focus on what looked like a rippling carpet beneath her. Further swearing as she vomited again. Then she was spun round, narrowly missing a door frame. The smell of oil and damp concrete, another close shave with a door, then cold air on her face and a dank wet odour she couldn't identify. Her senses sharpened and she could now smell newly mown grass and glimpse the outline of long legs pounding the ground in the midst of swirling clouds of clinging white vapour. They were outside – in a garden? Running through the mist? But why? And who was carrying her?

Then memory returned and with it the knowledge that she was going to die. He was taking her somewhere to kill her. She had to do something before it was too late. She tensed and tried to throw herself sideways to break the grip of the arm, which she could now feel encircling her waist, and had the satisfaction of making him stumble and almost go over on one knee. But he kept hold and she could hear his breath rasping as if through gritted teeth. 'Pack it in, you stupid bitch, unless you *want* to die.'

Something hard and sharp slapped her across the face and she glimpsed the skeletal branches of trees all around them. They were in a wood and she felt his feet crunching on gravel. A path? She raised her head and saw a building looming up through the mist. It looked like a barn of some sort and, as they drew closer, she saw that one of the big double doors was half open. Then they were through into a grey half-light and the smell of rotting straw assailed her nostrils.

Abruptly he stopped and she felt herself being swung around off his shoulder. His hands lingered on her hips as her feet touched the ground. 'Can you stand?' he snapped. She tensed and he gave a familiar bitter laugh. 'Don't worry, love. I'm not going to rape you.'

He released her and she stood there swaying for a moment before reaching out and grabbing his arm as her legs gave way. Her head was still spinning and she felt weak and disorientated.

'Lean on me,' he directed. 'We've got to find somewhere to hide before he realizes where we've gone.'

'It's Copely, isn't it?' she said, her voice still thick and almost incoherent.

'Well, it isn't the Archbishop of Canterbury,' he retorted and suddenly a powerful light blazed into life.

His torch was directed upwards to confirm his identity, giving the thin pale face, with its mop of unruly black hair, an almost waxen appearance.

'Satisfied?' he said. 'Now hurry. He went to get your car and he must be back by now, which means he'll know you've gone.'

Masking his torch in his hand, he led the way past rusted farm machinery to the rear wall of the barn, beneath the overhang of a hayloft, then pushed her in between an old reversible plough and a partially stripped tractor.

'Et tu, Brute?,' Kate murmured, turning her head away from him as she brought up more bile and spat into the darkness.

He grunted. 'Took you long enough to work that one out, didn't it?' he admonished.

'So how did *you* find out it was Haslar?'

He sighed heavily. 'I started putting two and two together when I was on the run – had the time, you see – and realized that, with all that had been happening, it could only have been him. But I couldn't prove it. That's why I was lurking around the house just now – to see if I could find anything that would directly incriminate him. I thought the mist and the gathering dusk would give me some cover. Lucky for you I did! '

'I'll drink to that,' she said soberly. 'But exactly where are we?'

'Just on the edge of his property. Used to be a farm here at some time, I reckon but this barn looks as though it hasn't been used for yonks. I found the place after I had scarpered and I hid away here so I could keep an eye on Neville while I decided what to do about him.'

She started to say something but his hand suddenly gripped her arm tightly in warning and she froze. She'd just heard it too – the crunch of feet on gravel. Haslar was coming.

CHAPTER 25

'JUST GOT HERE, sir,' the uniformed sergeant announced, when he met Ansell and Roscoe in the driveway of Haslar's house. 'No one seems to want to answer the door and the place is locked up tighter than a duck's arse.'

Roscoe stared at the blue MX5 sports car parked halfway up the driveway behind a big black Mercedes. 'And that's Kate Lewis's car,' he commented grimly. 'Which means she's got to be around here somewhere.'

Ansell turned back to the uniformed sergeant. 'So what are you waiting for, Sergeant?' he rapped. 'Break the bloody door down!'

The uniformed man nodded and faded into the mist, shouting to his team as he went, leaving Roscoe to launch a savage kick at the tyre of the Mercedes in obvious frustration.

'That'll help a lot,' Ansell snapped sarcastically. 'Be more useful to check the boot, I think.'

The DI nodded, cottoning on to his meaning straightaway. They were in luck too – the keys were still in the car's ignition. But the beam of Roscoe's torch revealed that the boot contained no body, just a sack of what looked like straw and some clothing – and he was about to shut the lid again with a feeling of relief when Ansell stayed his hand.

‘What the devil’s all that?’ he exclaimed and bent down to examine the clothing more closely, impatiently gesturing Roscoe to switch on his torch again.

‘Well, I’ll be buggered!’ the DI exclaimed as his boss produced a floppy hat and a heavy-looking boot.

‘And the other boot and long tattered coat Miss Herbert described look like being there too,’ Ansell said grimly. ‘A little job for forensics to slot into their agenda first thing in the morning, I think.’

Roscoe stared about him in the mist again, his unease palpable. ‘Let’s hope Kate doesn’t end up on their agenda too, Guv,’ he commented grimly.

At that precise moment, Kate Lewis was doing her level best not to end up on anyone’s agenda and she held her breath as the powerful torch probed the barn from the half-open door, focusing on the derelict machinery at the far end before travelling up the wall to the hayloft beneath which Kate and Copely sheltered.

Footsteps squelched through the rotting straw, pausing every few seconds to direct the beam of the torch into every nook and cranny. She felt Copely tense beside her but his hand on her arm squeezed a further warning as the torch grazed the wheels of the tractor they were crouched behind and highlighted the wicked raised blades of the reversible plough before swinging sharply away to home in on a sudden scuffling sound – a rat perhaps – on the far side of the barn.

The footsteps moved away from the tractor, slowly, confidently, unhurried – the torch steady in Haslar’s hand. Kate caught a glimpse of his silhouette within the circle of light in which he moved and shivered. He looked even taller than he had before and, thinking of the people he had already killed so violently, she felt that the chances of Copely and herself being able to overpower him, even two on one, were virtually nil. And it was then that a sudden excruciating cramp in her thigh forced her to move her leg slightly to ease the pain. Already weak from the combined effects of the sedative and the whisky, she lost her balance and in an instant it was all over as she fell against a metal cover that looked to have been removed from the tractor and was now resting against one wheel. The loud 'clang' sounded deafening in the confined space and it galvanized Haslar into immediate action. Even as Copely jerked Kate to her feet with the intention of propelling her towards the open door of the barn, Haslar was on to them, cutting off their escape with great loping strides, the torch in his hand pinpointing them as they stumbled through the mounds of rotting straw.

Copely courageously pushed Kate behind him and swung his torch at Haslar's head but he was completely outclassed. The ex-army man simply sidestepped the blow and tore the thing from his grasp, hurling it into the gloom to one side of him, where it lay, still lit and pointing upwards, with its beam trained on the combatants like the super-trouper on a theatre stage. Then, as Copely shouted desperately to Kate to run, the two figures seemed to fuse into one and Kate heard a choking gasp. It was only when Copely sank slowly into the straw, his hands trailing down Haslar's chest and abdomen as if trying to find something to hold on to, that she saw the glint of the blade in the other's hand.

'No need to pretend any more, is there?' Haslar sneered, advancing towards her. 'And I'm as good with a knife as I am with my bare hands, I assure you.'

For a moment Kate found herself unable to move – just as a mouse is temporarily paralyzed by the gaze of a cobra – and she would probably have remained like that too, until Haslar's knife sliced into her, had not something happened to crash through the ice gripping her brain.

That something was a sudden commotion high up in the roof area of the barn and a ghostly white shape that swooped low over her head, almost parting her hair, then disappeared back into the vault with a single hooting cry. The owl's intervention was nothing short of providential, providing shock therapy that kicked in instantly and created an adrenalin surge that jerked her out of her trance-like state and sent her staggering back into the gloom.

She fell twice as she retreated to the back of the barn, tripping over the humps of rotting straw and other debris that littered the floor but Haslar made no effort to capitalize on the advantage this gave him – instead following her at the measured deliberate pace of a man who knows only too well that his prospective victim has nowhere to run to anyway.

And the futility of retreat became apparent to Kate within a matter of seconds when she collided with something behind her that brought her to an abrupt, painful halt.

Haslar released a soft chuckle and stopped a few feet away, the beam of his torch blinding her. 'Oh dear,' he taunted, 'the little bird has nowhere left to fly to.'

Kate felt behind her, expecting to touch a wall. Instead, her hand found a series of wooden struts – she had slammed into the loft ladder.

Turning with a panicky gasp, she made a grab for the rung that was just above her head, ironically aided by the beam of Haslar's torch, and, as her scrabbling foot found the lower rung, she hauled herself up the ladder with a reckless disregard for anything save the need to put distance between herself and the man with the knife.

Haslar seemed to find the whole thing even more amusing and his mocking laugh followed her. 'What's that old 1960s song, Kate?' he called out. 'You must have heard it.' He began softly singing, '"Where do you go to my lovely, when you're alone in your bed." Peter Sarstedt, wasn't it? Quite appropriate here, don't you think?'

Shrinking away from the edge of the loft, Kate heard the ladder creak as Haslar put his weight on it and, in spite of her predicament, she found her mind flashing back to what seemed like only yesterday and another barn in which she had hidden from Twister, during her first encounter with the murderous psychopath. Then she had escaped death by the narrowest of margins but her future looked pretty bleak this time.

Her hands scrabbled around in the gloom amongst the straw covering the loft floor, feeling for anything that might be suitable for use as a weapon but she found only sharp stalks that dug into her hands and foul-smelling animal excrement – possibly from rats. Then her gaze jerked upwards as the faint outline of Haslar's head and shoulders appeared at the top of the ladder.

She retreated further back into the loft on her hands and knees until her back was up against the wall and she could go no further.

'Ah, now there you are, Kate,' Haslar said, straightening up with his torch trained on her crouching figure. 'Bit of a waste of time coming up here, wasn't it? Nowhere to go and all that. Still, we can amuse ourselves, can't we?'

She shielded her eyes against the glare of his torch, trying to peer at him from under her cupped hand. 'What is it?' she blurted on impulse. 'An inadequacy thing? You can't get it up, so you kill instead?'

Even in the gloom she could see him stiffen. 'It's got nothing to do with sex, Sergeant,' he said. 'This is about gain and revenge, two of the oldest motives for murder—'

'So you say,' Kate cut in, 'but deep down, you know it's more than that, don't you? You're just another psycho, trying to hide from the truth. Erectile dysfunction can be treated, you know.'

He swore and his voice was trembling as he snapped back. 'I am not a psychopath or sexually inadequate. This was all planned as a business project and, had it not been for Fallow's blackmail attempt and your own interference, it would have gone off without a hitch.'

Kate sensed that she had touched a nerve and she stayed with it. 'That's not what the judge will say when he commits you to a secure unit for an indefinite stay. No insurance pay-out, just needles, electric shock treatment and lots of nice tablets.'

'I'm not mad, you stupid bitch. I know exactly what I'm doing.'

'They won't see it that way. A grown man dressing up as a scarecrow, going around strangling people? Try making that sound normal at Crown Court. Do you fancy Broadmoor or Rampton? Maybe they'll give you a choice.'

Kate had gone too far. She realized that too late and, as he suddenly lunged at her, she only just managed to throw herself to one side in time. She heard the blade of the knife screech along the breeze blocks that formed the lower part of the loft wall but managed to knock the torch from his grasp before he could recover his balance.

It was only a temporary reprieve, however, and even as she scrambled across the loft towards the ladder on her hands and knees, like a crab racing for the sea, she knew she would never make it. He grabbed her by the hair first, hauling her back and dumping her on the floor at his feet. Then, turning her over, he dropped to his knees, with his legs astride her thighs, and cupped her chin in one powerful hand. She felt the point of the knife in his other hand pressed against her Adam's apple. God help her, he was going to cut her throat.

As it turned out, he had other intentions. 'Sexually inadequate, am I?' he snarled and, bringing the knife downwards, sliced through the front of her blouse. 'I'll show you just how sexually inadequate I am!'

'They'll be able to trace you through your DNA,' she gasped as he ripped the blouse off her in pieces.

'No problem, *Sergeant*,' he sneered. 'They won't even find you, or that idiot, Copely. This is the Somerset Levels, my dear, with so many convenient bogs in which to dump you both that I'll be spoilt for choice.'

But Haslar had made a big mistake by allowing himself to be distracted from his original purpose and, with the knife no longer pressing against her throat, Kate was encouraged to make one last effort to survive. The fingers of her left hand had already discovered that she was lying only a few inches from the edge of the loft and, taking a deep breath, she found enough strength from somewhere to suddenly slam her hips up into him, at the same time twisting hard to her left. Haslar might have expected her to make a last-ditch attempt to defend herself by going for his nether regions or by trying to claw his face with her nails but he hadn't bargained for this kind of response. Caught completely off balance, he was thrown right across Kate's body on to one knee, dropping his knife in the process, and before he could recover, Kate's own knee had jabbed up into his crotch, sending him further on his way. Then, with arms flailing the air, he pitched head-first over the edge of the loft with a wild cry, which ended with a metallic crash and a bubbling scream of agony.

Grabbing his torch, which was still on, Kate crawled to the edge of the loft and peered over. Haslar had plunged directly on to the raised blades of the reversible plough she and Copely had sheltered behind, impaling himself on them like a barbecue pig stuck on a spit. He was still alive, lying there on his back twitching fitfully and staring up at her with what seemed like an expression of shock and disbelief but as the volume of blood pumping out of his ruptured arteries reduced, Kate turned away from the grisly sight.

Retrieving the remains of her blouse from the floor, she did her best to draw it around herself and waited a few moments for the inevitable. She heard Haslar's death rattle even from where she was sitting but couldn't bring herself to descend the ladder to the floor of the barn to check that he was truly gone.

Only when the place was suddenly illuminated by several flashlights and she heard Roscoe's belligerent voice shouting 'Kate, are you there?' did she make her move and leave the loft but she gave the reversible plough a very wide berth and hardly felt the DI draping his own coat over her shoulders as she was led out of the barn into the cold misty night.

Ansell was waiting for her in front of a knot of uniformed police officers but, even as he stepped forward to speak to her, he was outmanoeuvred by another more substantial figure who hobbled across in front of him, leaning on a walking stick.

‘Let’s get you home, Kate,’ Hayden said authoritatively, guiding her back along the gravel path and ignoring the smouldering look Ansell threw after them. ‘Everything here can wait until later.’

She gave a weak smile. ‘Think I scored this time, Hayd?’ she whispered.

He grinned as he threw open the door of his Jaguar. ‘Scored?’ he echoed. ‘Oh, you did that all right, old girl. But next time you decide to go flying off into the night, do try not to ruin our carpet with a glass of my best 2004 Barolo, OK?’

AFTER THE FACT

KATE RECEIVED A round of applause when she walked into the incident room the next day, her colleagues standing up with beaming smiles and loud cheers the moment she appeared. Even Roscoe looked less miserable than usual and his boot-button eyes gave her a critical once-over as she pushed through the half-open door of the SIO's office.

'Recovered then?' he said brusquely.

She nodded and sat down on a nearby chair without asking. 'How's Maurice Copely?' she queried, concern etched into her expression.

He scowled. 'Nasty stomach wound and the hospital have had to take out his spleen but he'll be OK apparently.' There was no sense of relief in his tone and his expression seemed to add a silent 'unfortunately'.

'He saved my life,' Kate said, giving him a hard stare.

He grunted, plainly unimpressed by that fact. 'So it seems, but I still reckon he did those girls in the Thames Valley.'

'Ancient history now, Guv,' she pointed out. 'Time to move on.'

He started to chew on his gum again, ignoring her comments. 'And you were a bloody idiot going to Haslar's place on your own anyway – not that he'll be bothering us any more in the morgue.'

She treated him to a rueful smile. 'Thanks for your concern for my welfare, Guv,' she replied. 'It's nice to know someone cares.'

The mouth under the Stalin moustache quivered slightly as the slab-like face registered the start of a lopsided grin but it was soon gone. 'What do you expect – a medal?' he growled. 'Still, it's all over now, thank God, and at last we'll be able to get rid of these MCIU twats from headquarters when the incident room closes down in a few days.'

Kate raised her eyebrows, glancing quickly behind her. 'I don't think Mr Ansell would like being called an MCIU twat, Guv,' she pointed out. 'He might see it as just a little bit demeaning.' She glanced over her shoulder into the main incident room and back again. 'And where *is* Mr Ansell? I thought he'd be here by now. The debrief is in ten minutes.'

Roscoe gave a lingering grin. 'Oh, he'll be joining us at some stage,' he replied. 'Once he gets back from the big house, that is.'

She threw him a quizzical glance. 'Headquarters? Why is he there again? To shout the good news about his fantastic single-handed detection?'

'Not exactly.' Roscoe leaned forward conspiratorially. 'I shouldn't really be telling you this but I know it won't go any further. It seems a young female member of Mr Ansell's own clerical staff has made a complaint of sexism against him.'

'Bloody hell! And?'

'And, as soon as he finishes up here, he's being sent on an Equal Opportunities course at the force training centre – and that's not all.' Roscoe could hardly contain himself. 'When he gets back, he's being transferred from headquarters CID to Superintendent, Roads Policing.'

'Traffic? You mean he's going to become a black rat?'

'If that's what they call Traffic nowadays, yes.'

Kate was also grinning now. 'How appropriate,' she replied. 'And it couldn't have happened to a more deserving person.'

He flicked his bushy brows and shrugged. 'Thought you might be interested in that little snippet,' he said and turned towards the door. 'Anyway, in the absence of Mr Ansell, I'd better get this debrief started.'

He was almost through the door when he stopped and, snapping his fingers, swung round again. 'Oh, by the way, there's an envelope on the desk there for you.'

'For me?'

'Yeah, brought up from the postroom earlier. Hand delivered apparently. Probably some missive from the press—' He gave another faint smirk '– or a present from an admirer. It's marked In Confidence so I didn't open it.'

Then, heading into the main incident room where uniformed and plainclothes officers were already gathering and securing seats for themselves, he called back over his shoulder, 'Five minutes to briefing, don't forget.'

Kate sighed and crossed to the desk, picking up the A5-size padded envelope which was lying there and staring at it curiously. Her name was scrawled across the front in bold block capitals, plus the address, MCIU Highbridge Police Station but nothing more, and, though it appeared to contain something bulky, it was quite light. She frowned, weighing it in one hand. Hardly something from the press. As for admirers – and she snorted – the only one she was interested in was at home with a bad back!

She heard Roscoe's voice shouting from the incident room, 'OK, you lot, listen up,' as she slid a biro under the flap of the envelope and tore it open but then all sounds merged into one distant unreal hum as she shook what was in the envelope out on to the desk. There wasn't a missive of any kind inside the envelope or what could be termed a present – just a grotesque straw doll with a set of metal sergeant's stripes pinned neatly to its chest. And as she stood there, frozen to the spot with shock, the branch of an old hawthorn tree stretching over the wall of the police station yard from the derelict garden next door scraped across the office window in a sudden inexplicable breeze.

THE END

the Detective Kate Hamblin mystery series

Book 1: MURDER ON THE LEVELS
Book 2: REVENGE ON THE LEVELS
Book 3: FEAR ON THE LEVELS
Book 4: KILLER ON THE LEVELS

Please join our mailing list for updates on DETECTIVE KATE HAMBLIN, free Kindle crime thriller, detective, mystery books and new releases.

http://www.joffebooks.com/contact/

Thank you for reading this book. If you enjoyed it please leave feedback on Amazon, and if there is anything we missed or you have a question about then please get in touch. The author and publishing team appreciate your feedback and time reading this book.

Please join our mailing list for free kindle crime thriller, detective, mystery, and romance books and new releases. http://www.joffebooks.com/contact/

Our email is office@joffebooks.com

http://joffebooks.com

We hate typos but sometimes they slip through.
Please send any errors you find to corrections@joffebooks.com

We'll get them fixed ASAP. We're very grateful to eagle-eyed readers who take the time to contact us.

Printed in Great Britain
by Amazon

35158498R00121